**Bonnie Etherington** was born in Nelson, New Zealand, but spent most of her childhood in West Papua, and her experiences there inspired her first novel. Currently, she lives with her husband and cat in Chicago, where she is working towards a PhD at Northwestern University, focusing on tropical ecologies in Southeast Asian and Oceania literatures. She was shortlisted for the Commonwealth Short Story Prize in 2016, and has had poetry, short fiction and travel writing published in literary magazines and anthologies in Australia, New Zealand, the United States and Malaysia. She was shortlisted for the BNZ Katherine Mansfield Award in 2013, and named *AA Directions* New Travel Writer of the Year in 2011.

# THE EARTH CRIES OUT

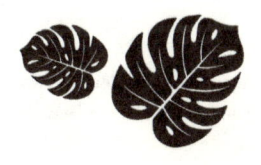

**BONNIE ETHERINGTON**

**VINTAGE**

VINTAGE

UK | USA | Canada | Ireland | Australia
India | New Zealand | South Africa | China

Vintage is an imprint of the Penguin Random House group of companies, whose addresses can be found at global.penguinrandomhouse.com.

Penguin Random House New Zealand

First published by Penguin Random House New Zealand, 2017

10 9 8 7 6 5 4 3 2 1

Text © Bonnie Etherington, 2017

The moral right of the author has been asserted.

All rights reserved. Without limiting the rights under copyright reserved above, no part of this publication may be reproduced, stored in or introduced into a retrieval system, or transmitted, in any form or by any means (electronic, mechanical, photocopying, recording or otherwise), without the prior written permission of both the copyright owner and the above publisher of this book.

Cover design by Sarah Healey © Penguin Random House New Zealand
Text design by Rachel Clark © Penguin Random House New Zealand
Author photograph © Josh Eastwood
Prepress by Image Centre Group
Printed and bound in Australia by Griffin Press, an Accredited ISO AS/NZS 14001 Environmental Management Systems Printer

A catalogue record for this book is available from the National Library of New Zealand.

ISBN 978-0-14377-065-7
eISBN 978-0-14377-066-4

The assistance of Creative New Zealand towards the production of this book is gratefully acknowledged by the publisher.

creative nz
ARTS COUNCIL OF NEW ZEALAND TOI AOTEAROA

penguin.co.nz

MIX
Paper from responsible sources
FSC® C009448

For my parents, and for
my mothers and fathers in Papua

We know that everything on the
earth cries out with pain, the same as
a woman giving birth to a child.

*— Romans 8:22,* NLV

## IN THE BEGINNING
*Nelson, New Zealand*

Here Julia and I are, down by the creek below the yellow house the last summer she is with us. Picking at sandfly bites on our shins, our hair damp and coiled on our necks. Hair cut short like boys' because it is easier for our mother, and our father says it will keep the devil and bad men away. I, eight, and knowing all about what can lurk in the smooth depths. Julia, five, already wanting to see. Both of us shocking ourselves in the cold, knees hunched to our chests, curling against thoughts of dark bodies of eels slipping down in the darker and darker green. Flat grey rocks in the sun where we lie like chicken thighs bumped together in a pan, burning pink patches on our backs, then jumping into the water to shock ourselves pale again.

Warm skin, cool milk in glass bottles, the bees in the weeds.

In the days while we waited for Julia to die, and before my father decided that atonement was in order and the mountains of Irian Jaya were just the place to find it, I sat for hours behind the bathroom block at school, poking a stick into a decades-old bullet hole in the concrete wall. Playground wisdom said that hole could have been caused by practically anything. Stray hunter's shot, target practice, murder.

An accident, they said, when they talked about what happened to Julia: the social worker, the police, the doctors who all wore the same brand of brown leather shoes. And of course it was, but when a five-year-old dies it is like a plane crash, a hit-and-run. It is easier if there is someone to blame.

The children at school blamed the taniwha that lived below Mr Ashton's vineyard. The newspapers blamed Common Household Hazards and Parental Negligence. The pastor and the fat ladies wrapped in florals at church blamed The Fallen World, and probably The Breakdown of the Nuclear Family. Our dad blamed Miriam, our mother, because she was not there when the flames first caught. Our mother blamed him (and maybe, partly, me) because at that time she blamed Dad for her whole life, and Julia dying was just part of the package.

Julia burned and it took three days for her to die. Like Jesus, I thought then, only later I realised I had the story backwards. Besides, Jesus did not burn. When Julia's nightgown caught a flame from the fireplace, there was a rush of heat and sparks like fireflies. Too-black eyes in a white, white face. The quilt our grandmother gave our mother on her wedding day. The smell of melted plastic, charred wool and something else, something I still do not know how to name.

One day the yellow house held Julia's voice, and then it did not. One day I was a sister, and then I was not. One day we were in a dream world, where Julia was dead and the space where she once was became large and silent, and then we were in another country altogether — where stories and voices made their way into our house any way they could. They heaved under the floorboards, whispered in the windows. Creaked in the attic like a python grown too big on rats. And I collected them all to fill that silence Julia left. At first it was like I was grasping at fireflies and could only catch one at a time. But, as my body grew with all these stories, as my mouth widened to fit other languages inside, I tried to collect more and more. And I was afraid, so afraid, of even one voice escaping and being lost forever — like Julia's voice that was in my ear for five years, then gone. Now I am older and my body can no longer hold them all, so I have started compiling scraps and fragments of what I remember, what I kept. This is why we have this book.

Before we left Nelson, my grandfather came to the yellow house and gave me two books. The first was a guide to the flora and fauna of New Guinea. Maybe this will give you something to write to me about, he said. Tell me what you see. We looked through the pages together. We practised saying the scientific names. I liked the parts about the plants best because they were so brightly coloured. It was hard to imagine the animals and flowers on those pages becoming a part of my own world. They looked like things that could only belong on pages or on a screen. The second book was *The Swiss Family Robinson*. It had a picture of a shipwreck on the front and, in the background, a zebra and human silhouettes against palm trees. In that book there was a mother who wasn't like my mother at all and a father who was someone I think my father would have liked to be. Be glad you're not going by ship, my grandfather said. Thus armed, he could send me anywhere.

My grandmother gave me a dream-catcher like the ones in her spare room that my dad called cheap hippy nonsense (and even Grandma said she did not really know what they were for and she liked them only because the sixties happened and her ones were easy to make). Julia and I used to play with them during visits. Grandma made the one she gave me out of blue wool and brown twine, feathers dipped in gold paint hanging from its round belly. She said that this way we would be connected like the way the wool reaches out and wraps around its hoop. Julia always liked to make the feathers swing. Dad used to come with us on those visits, to share a beer and biscuits with my grandfather and talk about the apples, but Mum would have washing to do, a floor to vacuum, a headache to get rid of. Tell her we send our love, Grandma used to say. We always did and Mum always said she'd come with us Next Time, which is a time that is stuck in the future, always right before you so you can see it but not reach it.

In our old-new village house, I would hang the catcher above my bed and wonder if the dreams it caught were the ones already in my head, going out into the world after they were finished, or if they were dreams that were trying to find their way to me. I know now that dreams and plants have something in common — you can try to make them do what you want, but you cannot know exactly how they will turn out. They have lives of their own. That is why I prefer dreams and plants to histories. Histories are too much about joining the dots. Dreams and plants are about living, with histories still growing through them.

Twenty years later, the guidebook's pages and spine have subsided under the weight of my amendments to its entries, the stuffing of extra pages in between chapters, the torn-out pages from when I understood everything that was missing from them. It was never made to hold all the stories, all the voices, not even all of the plants and animals. I left Irian Jaya while still a child, but returned twice — once as an adolescent and once as an adult. The stories I collected then supplement the earlier memories. Now, in another country, in greenhouses, I grow the plants I first saw in the guidebook pages. Banana, papaya, tea tree, all manner of orchids. Breadfruit, fern, hibiscus, palm. I have hope that the bodies of plants and of animals and of people hold stories and possibilities better than books ever can — possibilities for both Julia and the land once called Irian Jaya. But, all the same, I cannot help myself from trying to order both Julia and what is now Papua in these pages. Even as I can feel them slipping away from me, multiplying out of control.

This telling is supposed to be a kind of healing, though it will not be able to tell everything and it might not always look like a healing — just as a wound's pre-scab cell bloom masks its own growth. I will show the shine on our mother's hair after she washes it on a frosted Sunday night before we leave for that village called Yuvut in the mountains, a village that is not even named on most maps. Show the curve of an orchid petal fallen in the thick syrup water that collects in the hollows of a rotting stump. Show how the body of a lost plane sinks and crumbles like a once living thing. Paint the clouds that gather in pillars above a jungle's impossible glaciers, hot air meeting cool. Give smoke on a tongue, sweat on the backs of knees, the voice of an unseen bird dripping through the forest canopy like water.

When we flew on the plane towards Irian Jaya that first time, I looked at its body on those maps you get in the inflight magazines so I could trace how far we had come and how far there was still to go. The island of New Guinea has a bird's body, the body of the most important bird on the island — the bird of paradise. The head and chest belong to Irian Jaya, which was then and still is today part of Indonesia but reincarnated under another name. The rest of the torso and tail belong to Papua New Guinea, which is a different country even though nothing but a thin black line separates it from its other half.

Later I read in my guidebook how Malay traders visiting the edges of New Guinea called the bird of paradise *burung mati*, the dead bird. Because it was so beautiful, all they ever saw of it was the feathers or the skins prepared to be sold all in a row or mounted on someone's headdress. But I did not see a dead bird when I looked at that bird's body on the long flight. It looked like it was ready to grow wings and fly away, right out of my magazine pages. It did not look like it was supposed to be stuck there above Australia with no way to escape. It looked alive. It looked like it could shake itself free and tear its feathers from the blue grasping sea. It looked wide-mouthed and angry.

# ONE

We arrived in Irian Jaya, Indonesia, in 1997 with hard-shelled suitcases, extra locks, and a crate of cheap eyeglasses donated by a non-profit to spread as we saw fit. We arrived with pamphlets on AIDS, dysentery, malaria, tuberculosis — all in a language that neither we nor the people we would live with could speak. We arrived with avocado seedlings wrapped in old rice sacks, and twenty-three live baby rabbits in cardboard boxes that used to package two-minute noodles. In the white-tiled Bali airport, before the last flight to Irian Jaya, I could see a black-spotted ear poking out of one of the holes Dad made with his pocketknife so that the rabbits could breathe.

Out we tipped from the plane, lurching forward with the weight of our bags. Out into the glare of sun on tarmac. We were in a world that trapped us like flies under an upturned glass, waiting for a magnified beam of sunlight to scorch us like grass.

There were vans the drivers called taxis, all in a row, lined up in front of the airport. Two children pressed their faces against the car-park fence and stared at me. I stared back. One wore a shirt that advertised FREE KONDOMS and a happy smile.

I don't know where to look, said Mum. I wasn't sure if she was talking about the shirt or something else. We got into one of the vans, pressed our legs into broken vinyl seats. Apart from the seats, the interior of the van had no panels or linings like I was used to seeing in cars — it was gutted, a shell in the heat.

The air was swollen. In it everything seemed to float as if suspended on an invisible fishing line: the noon call to prayer, the scents of clove cigarettes and petrol, spits of grease as bananas fried in a roadside cart, an old man with his shirt off selling watermelons and papayas under a tree. Sweat on his nipples. I counted crumpled soft-drink cans and plastic bags caught in power lines, in trees. Motorcycles poured from every direction on to the streets, like ants boiling from a nest. There was one traffic light that flashed pink for stop and blue for go. No one paid it any attention. A woman fanned herself by a cart of glass Pepsi bottles filled with liquid the colour of dehydrated pee. Later I would know these bottles were filled with petrol for the motorcycles that lined up for hours.

This is Sentani, Dad told me, named for the wrinkle-free lake that feeds the clusters of rusted houses on stilts that crop up on its shore. Our door into the jungle, into the mountains that rose far off in the distance under heavy clouds. I wondered how clean the jungle was in Dad's mind, how untouched like the cream that rises to the surface of raw milk. Somehow, I already knew he would be disappointed.

Look, Ruth, a hornbill, said Mum. She let go of the bag she clutched so tight to point for me. There were patterns from the seat on the backs of her arms. The bird she pointed at wandered along small tin-roofed shops that sold potato chips and lollipops. A bit of red string trailed from one of its legs. Dad smiled and went on trying to talk to the driver in English.

Have you lived here long? he asked.

Here? said the driver. Oh no, no, no.

You're from somewhere else then?

Yes, yes, yes. I want to go to America. Bring back lots of money. Why you only have one child? Have older ones, yes?

No, just a daughter.

One. Singular. No 's' tacked on the end. A youngest daughter erased as easily as a single letter.

The driver sucked the air between his teeth. You have a son? Yes. Don't worry.

Dad gave up. A burst of fluorescent green hugged the base of the mountain watching over all of this, over all of us.

Mount Cyclops, said our driver, only he said it like Siiklop. Still, this was a word I knew, a word that came complete with illustrations of Greek mythology in a corner of free-reading time during some past slow school day. Grey beards, a flowing tunic. I looked for the single eye and saw only a waterfall, weeping white.

'Community development' was scribbled on our visas. Dad could build things, could plant things. Things like a village hospital, like avocado trees. Mum could mother and hand out whatever she was given. Glasses, rabbits, pamphlets. We would run a breeding programme with the rabbits. They would multiply and so would the avocados. We would fill village bellies with protein, turn malnutrition into smiles. It was all in the letter that Dad was given in a shining Wellington office. It was all in the brochures that promised this would make us good.

It *will* be good for us, Dad told Mum late one night in the yellow house. Dad had always meant to do something like this, something like helping people, or so he said. Now was their chance, at a time when their lives, our lives, were all up in the air, floating like lost dandelion seeds hoping to land somewhere sure and firm. I listened to my parents while squatting in the shadows of the hall when I should have been in bed. Dad, going to the kitchen to put the kettle on for tea, must have seen me there but he didn't tell. He went back to her chair and held Mum's hand.

It won't be for long, but it will give us something to do. We have to do something.

It feels like forgetting, said Mum. And this doesn't change anything.

Not forgetting. We're making the best out of a bad thing.

One year, said Mum.

Government contractors were building a road from the town nearest to our assigned village, according to the man who met us at the guesthouse in Sentani with fried snacks for my parents, hard coffee-flavoured lollies for me. A road that would cut through the mountains like they weren't there, forge rivers, smooth hills. It would meet Dad at the hospital in two, maybe three years. Five years tops, the man said. He wore a uniform, but I couldn't tell what kind of uniform it was and his accent didn't fit the accents I knew either, though he looked Indonesian. Here, things and people did not fit easily into the categories I used to have.

Six years at most, if things really turn to custard. All Dad had to do was meet that road with his hospital.

Dad did the talking with the man. He winked at Mum now and then. One year, said his eyelid going down. One year. Don't worry.

They told me not to smile when we went to get our visa photos taken against a red velvet drape that the camera would turn a faded grey. Looking at them made me think of Julia's dresses, her tee-shirts, and how already I could not always remember what colours they were. Dad collected rows of headshots for all of us in his money pouch. Paperwork sprouted as much as trees in that place.

We went to the police station and gave the police our fingerprints. There was no running water at the station to wash the ink off our hands, so we wiped them on Dad's shorts. They'll be my new-old work shorts, he said. The policemen liked to watch Mum, hold her hand too long when they pressed her fingers into the inkpads and then onto the paper.

Dutch New Guinea, West Irian, Irian Jaya, West Papua. The name of this province changed (and still changes). Its history is one of invasions and divisions. Everyone hungry for a piece of 'Java's Kitchen'. Take some sandalwood here, some oil there, and don't forget the gold and copper. Dad told me about the big invasions (the Dutch, the explorers, the Americans and Japanese and Australians in the Second World War, the missionaries, the miners, the Indonesian Army). He told me about the man called Suharto in Java, and how he once was a general who took power in the middle of the night. It was Suharto who was President in 1969, when Indonesia officially grew by over 162,000 square miles, thanks to Papua. The United Nations had a conversation, men in offices drew lines, and the front half of New Guinea's bird body remained separated from its back half, its sweeping tail, because the Indonesian Army had guns and friends, and the men in offices thought that Papua's bird mouth would never open and speak for itself. And it was Suharto who, in 1997 (the man would not die!), still held Papua in his hand.

Over time I learned of the smaller invasions, too. I learned about the weaver ants that hitchhiked into the highlands in sugar sacks. From an airport hangar they spread outwards, forever marching downhill. African snails were brought into the swamp regions. Like a wave, they guzzled everything green. Back in the highlands again, Australian missionaries brought lantana with them in the 1970s, and vegetables in abandoned gardens were gently strangled. After small Cessna aeroplanes started servicing the Mamberamo (that region where rivers snake across the landscape like trails of some impossibly large creature), walking catfish appeared and multiplied. And then there were the macaque monkeys that made their homes in colonies near the coast after transmigrants brought them there from other Indonesian islands. Overseas animal rights activists insisted that they be left alone rather than shot. Because, after all, they did not ask to be migrants themselves. Whole (human) transmigrant camps relocated (yet again) as they escaped from the thievery of the monkeys.

Then came rabies; now comes AIDS. Men with government badges shipped prostitutes, HIV-positive, to Papua. Look at Java! Free of AIDS! They gloated while health workers in Papua told villagers that only bad people get AIDS so they were safe, they were fine, they could spread their money, spread their legs.

Some people thought the land of Papua was dying. They thought its earthquakes that sent the bird's head into spasms and its rivers bleeding copper were its aggressive death throes. But we thought it looked like the most living land we had ever seen. We thought this meant we could come alive again here, too.

## BREADFRUIT
*No Man's Land, 1944*

*Native to New Guinea, and spread by early Melanesians and Polynesians to many other parts of the South Pacific, Southeast Asia and Central America, breadfruit is the much larger cousin of the mulberry tree. It produces large green fruit, with white or yellowish starchy insides. It is so high in nutrition (though bland) that in the eighteenth century Europeans transported it to the West Indies, intending to use it to feed slaves on the sugar plantations. Mutineers on HMS* Bounty *threw hundreds of kilograms of it overboard to float away on the Pacific.*

*Breadfruit, the travelling fruit. When I grow them now, I am always amazed by how fast their trees grow, and how light the wood is even though the fruit is so heavy. It did not take me long to learn its shapes, its weights. But other things about Papua took a lot longer to know and, even then, only in fragments that never fully fitted together except in my imagination. For example:*

*Once upon a time, when the Second World War filled the Pacific with metal and hidden corpses, the island of New Guinea was not as forgotten by the rest of the world as it is now. The jungles were filled with Japanese and malaria (according to the newspapers), and the Americans camped out by the coast as they sweated in their tents and wondered about the people they called cannibals hidden in the mountains. They named some of the mountains and rivers, not thinking they already had names given to them by others. Perhaps they tried breadfruit.*

*Some of you may have heard of the US flight that went down in one mountain valley. That valley was christened Shangri-La by the white people who (like so many white people) came and went and later got to speak the stories without any say-so from the people they filled their stories with. This story isn't about that plane. Enough have talked about that one. This story is about another plane, one that wasn't found, with no rescue story to splash under a big headline in an American or Australian newspaper, and therefore no happy ending. Only a brief note documenting its loss in the war effort. One moment its radio was connected to another across airwaves (as unstable as a deck of cards), another moment the connection was lost and that was that. For the rest we have to fill in the blanks.*

*There were three people on board this plane. John Carlos Mendoza and Mervin Salazar were from the Philippines. Both joined the US Army as paratroopers to fight under General MacArthur. John Carlos piloted the plane, with Mervin as his navigator. Michael Pugawak was the third person aboard. The other two were returning him to his village in the mountains after he had helped them map areas where the Japanese might be hiding.*

*The three had time, maybe a few seconds, in between the plane going down and the plane hitting the ground to realise that it was going to crash. Perhaps John Carlos thought of paperwork he hadn't finished and the damp scent of his mother. Michael, named for an early Dutch priest who had made it to his village the week he was born, might have thought of the strangeness of clouds when viewed from above rather than below. And how was it that the river below was so close already? I imagine that Mervin thought of the light coming through the windows of his church back home and too many missed confessions.*

*There was no rescue mission launched when radio control determined that the plane was lost.*

*The location of the crash was too high and too far from the US base in Hollandia, and altogether too close to real or imagined Japanese hideouts. So, on official documents at least, that is the end of the story of the flight. Mervin's girlfriend named her first son (to a different man) after him, and John Carlos's grandmother confirmed that it was true planes took people to Heaven and never returned them. As for Michael's family? They weren't surprised that he never returned. But they didn't stop watching the skies either. Their (relatively newly coined) word for plane mimicked the sound they heard when military ones passed in the distance, or the two times one had landed on the small strip cleared next to some gardens a three-day walk away. Wuru wuru wuru. The sound of blades against air, of wings that don't beat.*

*Michael's body fell near a breadfruit tree and rotted along with its fallen fruit. This is how you choose a good breadfruit to eat, his mother told him as a child. Its skin will be cracked a little. Maybe there will be some dried sap. And you will be able to smell it and feel that the flesh is as smooth as a girl's neck.*

# TWO

Aren't you a brave girl to go to such a faraway place? said the pastor's wife at church the day before we left New Zealand.

I'm not sure, I said. Because I hadn't thought about being brave yet or why it would be something I should need to be. She laughed like I was funny.

We stood up at the front of the church and people came around us and prayed. They prayed our mission would be successful. That God would bless it and that we would bring glory to Him. This made me feel like an astronaut going to the moon. Even though other things seemed to be getting mixed up with God here. The people praying stood so close I could smell their breakfasts, cigarettes and the angry layers of different perfumes. My mother was there with us, but she was quiet, and after the praying I saw her sitting in the church's rose garden, staring at her feet. She did not go to church much before Julia died. But on this day she did not say anything about not going. Just picked out skirts for herself and me, though forgot her favourite lipstick.

After all this family has gone through, said a man to Dad. He meant what happened to Julia. You're an inspiration to us all.

Well, when you feel called, said Dad. It was a phrase I had heard other people at church say before they did something that changed their lives, something that always meant them leaving and (in my memory) never coming back. Instead their family photos would be posted on the church bulletin board, next to a map with a coloured pin marking where they went: Togo, Bangladesh, Thailand, Albania, Japan. Sometimes we would pray for them in church and then there would be a special collection for them during the offering. We weren't going to be called missionaries like those people, Dad told me. Our job was only to bring aid, though God coming with us was a bonus. Because being missionaries meant more training and rules than we had time for. Dad just wanted to pack our bags and go.

After the church service, and before boarding the plane, nothing seemed to wipe the smile from Dad's face, but it didn't seem like a good smile. It was as if he was afraid he would run away and fail if he stopped smiling. I wondered if I should feel like running away, too, but I did not know where I would run.

---

There was what was true and what I only thought was true about Julia dying, and I tried to sort out which was which. Piles of facts on one side, piles of possibilities on the other. But they overlapped and crossed, wouldn't let themselves be neatly divided. There was the creek in summer, and the incident at the bend in the bigger river, but those came well before the accident, even though (for me) the images of water and fire will forever be connected by guilt. Mum was out with friends when It happened: asking questions about how to divide a house, throwing around the word Divorce like a leaking hacky sack. She wore the pearl earrings that she always wore when she wanted to look powerful and more sophisticated than she really was.

Dad was out the back of the house, working on his biggest cabinet yet: one with cherrywood and stained-glass panels built into the double doors, a single fantail on each. He broke glass on purpose so he could rearrange it into a better picture.

There was the grate, which should have been over the fire that Dad had just started lighting now the days were getting colder. But the grate was not in its place on that day.

There was that nightgown. That fight. One that was solid and proved, one whose words I will never quite remember. They will not be arranged. There were discussions about whether it would have been better, kinder if she had died quickly rather than slowly. But better, kinder for whom?

I have in my memory a list of the stories I told Julia when she was in the hospital. They are either true or things I wish I had said. In my head, sometimes my own thoughts and what is out loud become all the same —

Melissa from next door said she'd make a cake for you when you're better.

I'll help you catch up on your homework.

Jeremy F. said you're pretty and he likes you.

I'm sorry.

I love you.

Dad read to Julia from *Grimms' Fairy Tales*. In fairy tales, the eldest sister is always the evil one. The youngest is always blonde and good. She's the one who is supposed to have the happy ending.

Our parents met at a youth group meeting, or down by the beach while their friends did wheelies near the dunes, depending on which parent you asked. Either way, they both agreed that our mother wore a sky-blue dress and there were clouds, top heavy with sleet, gently tipping over the foothills.

Our mother, Miriam, was nineteen, and she wore a dress that day only because she had fought with our grandmother about it and lost. She usually wore tight pants and cuffed them at the ankle. The dress was handed down from a distant cousin, and Grandma Rose wouldn't let Mum get rid of it until she had worn it at least once. Miriam worked as a bank teller during the day and liked to spend her nights listening to The Who while reading philosophy books she didn't understand. She never planned to marry and thought that nineteen was too old to be bossed around by her mother. Our father, Isaac, was twenty-three, a builder's apprentice; he read mainly newspapers (for the cartoons and garage sales) and didn't drink. Sometimes he went to church.

It's not that he is or was uptight, Mum told one of her friends once, while they were sitting on the back porch of the yellow house and Julia and I were on the driveway assembling a toy railway track we had been given for Christmas. Just a bit idealistic and naïve.

Mum also told us how Dad would bring her ice creams during the few months they were dating, every Sunday, despite it not even being summer. He would go to the dairy on the other side of town and then turn up at her place with melted streaks down his arms, all sorts of colours running together and sticking his shirt to his skin. He always bought two different flavours, just in case Mum didn't feel like one or the other on that particular day. He'd eat the one she didn't want. In exchange, she taught him how to smoke, menthols mainly, which shocked him before he decided the smell wasn't so bad. They sat in the back yard and blew smoke over the tomatoes struggling up in the vegetable garden. By the time I was born the cigarettes were gone.

After the wedding, Isaac and Miriam moved into the yellow house that her parents owned, and they, George and Rose, bought a split-level cottage down by the creek, just far enough away not to be seen from the window. Dad took over his father-in-law's orchards one by one as George grew weaker and more immersed in his books and sketches (the lifecycle of an apple tree, cross-section of flowers, repeated in charcoal and ink, over and over). Dad had dreams, once, of building houses for a living. Ones with white wide porches and the windows called Romantic. He ended up, in between apple harvests and pruning season, putting together cabinets and chairs in the shed behind the house for shipping to middle-class families in the cities. On good days he whittled toys for children. Little wooden cars, sheep, spinning tops. Once, a giraffe with an extra-long neck and crooked soldered spots.

There's no market for those kinds of things now though, he told me. Julia and I used to go to the shed and sit in the sawdust and watch him work. No one wants old-fashioned wooden toys any more.

I like to think they were happy in those early years of marriage, the newness making everything tender. Like fresh petals, like a dew-spun spider web in the morning. But perhaps that was the problem — that what we call love, what we call connection between two people, is frail, so easy to break. When I try to picture it, this is what I see: Mum drying plates in the kitchen, Dad listening to the weather report on the radio in the living room. Both illuminated by candlelight because those days on their orchard were the days of the generator and they turned it off early every night to save fuel. There is something about candlelight that invites fear and loneliness. Something about that sphere of bright, someone at the centre, holding on tight and not knowing what could be beyond the edges. In my mind the darkness between my mother and father widens, the lights of their candles never quite meet. In their separate worlds they are alone.

# THREE

There was no time to grab on to Sentani before we launched into the air again, this time in a six-seater red-and-white-striped plane that finally pushed us through the bank of clouds that surrounded the town. During the flight I rested my head against the side of the plane and the thrum of its engine vibrated all through me. I counted the water droplets that collected on the underside of the wings as they grew fat and fell. Sometimes there were breaks in the trees below us. A few trees fallen, a thatch- or tin-roofed house. Most of the time I could not see any roads leading to those houses. They seemed to just appear by themselves, born from clouds and trees. I did not see any people until we approached our destination, and then there were lines of silhouettes streaming out of the houses and pooling at the airstrip that was a streak of pale green against the darker green of everything that surrounded it.

The village was built on a plateau squeezed between mountains. Government maps split it into two because it sat on the border of two provinces that divided up the land like an uncooperative cheesecake. It was a problem area for the maps, but seen from above those inked lines did not seem to mean much. On one side of the village I could see the pale scratches of a path making its way to a river that glinted over limestone before thickening and darkening further downstream as it slowed and went around a bend. Later, I would know that the closest part of the river was further away than it looked from above. Everything was further away in the village, because there were no finished roads, no vehicles. Then I would count how long it took to get to the river on foot from our house (one hour in dry weather), and how many miniature mudslides and rock falls I must navigate around because the path there was dirt, like all the paths in this place. But, for now —

Children stuck their heads between the slats of the fence surrounding the airstrip as we touched down in the village called Yuvut. Waved at me as if they knew me. Grass cuttings drifted in the wind. When the plane's engine shut off, all that could be heard at first were the rabbits drumming their heels down in the bowels of the pot-bellied plane. Right beneath our feet.

Our belongings were pulled quickly from the plane and piled almost as if they did it themselves: the avocado saplings, the rabbits, the tools. And then the plane left. We were alone with our pile of things. Alone because I did not yet know the people coming up to greet us. Alone because it felt like no one was ever going to come and find us if the grass on the airstrip grew too long and swallowed us whole. Just as it did to some of the graves in the church cemetery in Nelson where we buried Julia. We planted a cherry sapling by the plaque that marked her grave the day before we left.

In spring it will be beautiful here, said Dad.

Who will keep the plaque shiny? I asked.

Mum brushed at the dust already spreading over its surface.

In the village we left sweat in droplets on the front porch of the house by the airstrip that had been empty since the last aid workers left three months earlier. Their project was selling the peanuts that the villagers grew, drawing business plans, seeing the money roll in. And they were meant to build the hospital, too. Only peanuts rolled out but no money came back, and stacks of wood for the hospital rotted in the mud while paperwork flew between the coast and the mountains. The men, who no one ever seemed to know the names of, the men with money, money men, never did sign anything.

Dust spun in the sunlight, hung there and glittered as we opened the door. The door was just a screen in a frame that was tearing around the edges. Every now and then there was a deep hum in one of the walls, and it wasn't until we saw the soft black body of a bee boring into the wood on the outside of the house that we knew why. The bees were bigger in Yuvut. As were the geckoes, a gummy pale green, the rats that we heard nesting above the ceiling, the cockroaches that nibbled the edges of a stack of ancient cookbooks by the stove.

It was built in the seventies, Dad said of the house. And hasn't really been fixed up since. He looked at Mum as if for approval or in apology, and she, too quickly, smiled.

The house was built on metre-high pylons to protect it from termites and floods. Through gaps in the floorboards I saw the eyes of chickens, which seemed to walk freely between our yard and the airstrip, looking back at me. Through gaps in the curtains I saw the eyes of the same villagers who greeted us at the airstrip looking back at me, too. I felt out of place, a malformed bead on a string of perfect spheres. Everything I could see outside came filtered through these curtains, these floorboards. The world seemed in pieces, in fractured sunlight.

Mum adjusted the glass louvres that lay in ranks over mesh windows that were supposed to keep out mosquitoes, handed me a cloth to wipe the dust from them. At least the wind can come right through, she said. Her face was damp, but with sweat not tears because those were all cried out in the first of our four flights to Yuvut, the one that left New Zealand behind. Dad, forever grateful that she got on the plane in the first place (even if I did not believe it would last), forever grateful that those divorce papers never got signed (at least, not yet), handed her tissues one by one, offered to buy her anything on the airline menu. You'll like it, he said. Think of the flowers I can get you. They'll be so much brighter than anything we see back home. So much bigger.

I don't want flowers, said Mum. But she let him buy her a chicken roll, ate it all. Sometimes you have to understand that everyone is just trying their best, she told me when Dad got up to use the bathroom. Even when they're doing it wrong.

The last people who lived in the house left things behind. Tins of spam and beans in the pantry. Bottles of malaria prophylaxis in the hall cupboards. Rat poison. Old *National Geographic* magazines under the couch. A psychology textbook under the bed that became mine. Mum counted the things in the pantry like they were provisions in a siege, and I stuffed the magazines and the textbook further out of sight so that they would be my secret that no one could take away.

An evacuation list was taped to the back of the pantry door. 'In case of civil or social unrest', it said. It told us that we were allowed:

One suitcase per family.

Two sets of clothes each.

Essential medicines and personal hygiene items. 'For example: heart medication, dental floss'.

One journal or diary each.

One Bible.

And (for children) one toy each.

I unpacked my two bears and one doll in my room. I imagined lining them up and interviewing them in order to choose who might win a place in the plane with me. I thought up reasons each one could be left behind. Brown Eyes, you smell weird. Matilda, there's that spot on your dress where some bubble gum got stuck. Patches, you're falling apart.

Night crept up and surprised us on that first day. Dad lit a single gas lamp. The fumes comforted me, a reminder of something from the past but I was not sure what. We ate protein bars, the first of the box we brought from our not-now home (Dad was worried about malnutrition already), and taro chips Mum bought from a Sentani supermarket because they looked partly familiar. Sitting around the lamp made me feel like we should all join hands and sing. How long had it been since we sat this close and ate? I looked at the spot where Julia could have sat.

I chewed on my protein bar as slowly as possible, making it a game to see how long I could make one nibble last until it dissolved in my mouth. The breeze kept blowing, always blowing. Through the screen windows, the cracks in the floor, gaps in the ceiling; through my clothes and (it felt like) through me.

Then I started to notice the ants. Ants with black-red bodies and long clear wings, flying in waves towards our one beacon of light. They, too, got through the windows, the walls. As soon as we noticed them they were everywhere, crawling down collars, up pants' legs, in the corners of our mouths.

Time for bed then, Dad said.

Wait, said Mum. I need to do something first.

She went to her suitcase, brushed ants off it, and took out a calendar: one with pictures of New Zealand on every page. That month's picture showed the white peaks of mountains framing sunlit dock, sunlit lake. It felt both out of place and throbbingly familiar, like the whiff of the yellow house, or even the whiff of something that was close to Julia that I caught when unpacking my pyjamas. Mum hung the calendar in the kitchen and made one half of a cross through the day's date with a purple felt-tip pen. Then she handed the pen to me.

Make the second half of the cross, Ruth. Every day, while we're here, I'll make the first half in the morning and you'll complete it at night. Then it will feel like we're getting somewhere. It's like counting down to Christmas.

Her voice had something wrong in it, something bright but too easily crumpled like a piece of aluminium foil. I wondered if the countdown to leaving the village was the same thing as a countdown to her leaving us, Dad and me. She smiled at me — Go on. So I completed the purple cross that banished the date into a day that had already happened. Dad shook his head but did not say anything. Then we washed the dirt off our feet with the bucket shower that he had filled earlier from the rainwater drums outside. The water was rust-coloured and smelled like old blood.

The ants whose dead bodies we crunched in the morning

before we remembered they were there, and the sight of mould, black-green, growing up the walls of the shower, made me believe that I was drowning. Suffocating. As if a pillow was held to my face and the torture my own tears.

# FOUR

Dawn in the village was not a silent or a soft thing. Sound here was thick as if touchable. As I came awake and as the sky became lighter, the sounds of Yuvut became less like a wall of tide engulfing me in the night, and more like pieces of glass I could hold and try to fit into a bigger picture, the way my father did with his stained-glass windows. With our first dawn in the village I could pick out the sounds of roosters crowing under the house, groups of women passing by our fence on the way to their gardens, the coughs of men lingering by the gate, waiting to catch a glimpse of the strangers. The two-way radio spat voiceless static by the dining-room table as my father switched it on. When I heard the radio I got up, sliding out from under the mosquito net. Later I would make it a game in the mornings to try to slide out while barely untucking the net at all.

My mother sat at the table, trying to figure out how much milk powder to add to the water (boiled for diseases, filtered just in case) so that we could eat breakfast. She wore a pink robe that fell slightly open over her chest. I wanted to draw it tight and cover her. Dad had already piled the plans for the hospital in front of him on the table, and stared at them while drinking instant coffee. He was ready to begin, and his leg tapped a rhythm under the table, making the whole thing shake.

Stop it, said Mum.

Magnesium deficiency, apparently, said my father.

You're just worked up.

I liked to see them like this again, arguing at the table. Before the accident it was like they were two bees circling a hive but never on the same side at the same time.

I sat at the table with one of the crocheted blankets my grandmother sent with us over my legs, my toes curling against the air that rose from between the floorboards, remembering frost. Outside the fog was lifting from the airstrip as sunlight slid its way into the valley. I couldn't see the mountains yet, but I knew they were there, leaning close.

The milk was watery and had lumps of undissolved powder in it. Just drink it anyway, said Mum. I'll try to figure it out tomorrow. She constantly moved between kitchen and dining room, but for what I was not sure. She tried to switch on the kettle that sat on the plywood bench, forgetting it wasn't electric like the one at home.

Damn it, she said, coming back into the dining room, I didn't pack my nail polish. You know the coral one I like? But she didn't expect an answer because she kept walking past us to the window, making sure the dusty lace day curtain was covering it properly to blur our shapes inside, whether people were watching or not.

Flowers! Mum said then. We need flowers in this place! She slipped out of the house and quickly cut some from the bush by the porch as if she were ashamed, didn't want to be seen. A muscle in her neck was held tight, like she was holding back from something, just like it was when she stood in the doorway of Julia's room at the hospital, and just like it was when my father worked late, when they fought, when Julia and I told her we hated her and that she did not love us, really. But we knew we were lying as the words came out of our mouths. She always looked ready to run away, like a hummingbird hovering over one blossom, even if she never actually did. But now, with Julia gone, I did not know if I was ever going to be enough to keep her still.

Then, just as quick, she was back in the house again, slipping off her sandals so fast that the house rocked on its pylons. I dug my fingers into my seat, but even this didn't steady me.

Mum put the flowers in an empty jam jar and then tried to find all the little black ants burrowing between the flower petals, hunting for sweetness. But no matter how many she picked out, the ants bubbled up and multiplied again, pouring from the petals on to the table. The flowers were tiny, red and orange, packed in tight clusters. They didn't smell sweet like I thought they should, but instead smelled like crushed grass and made my eyes itch.

Shit, said my mother when she saw my eyelids swelling shut. I'll get the Benadryl. Dad shifted in his seat. He hated it when she swore. This was only the start of the allergies, though. The dust, the pollen, the mould, everything in Yuvut began a war with me. After a couple of weeks I got used to my skin vaguely itching always.

On this first morning my father was filled with energy. Energy in his leg tapping under the table, in his finger tapping on top of the radio. He ordered new wood to build the hospital, ticked off that task in a big green ledger that would sit on the coffee table all year for him to go over at night. People in the city warned him that he might be sold wood that the termites like to eat. This was the trick the people of Yuvut liked to play on the government workers, the outsiders, because in a few years the government buildings (schools, clinics, offices, homes for people who did not look the same as the people from Yuvut) would be sawdust and rot while the village huts still stood. So my father wrote out exactly what kind of wood he wanted to buy. He had done his research. When he was ready, he stood on the front porch and gave his instructions with a drawing and many gestures. The men hoping to go out and find the wood and bring it back to him nodded. But we had no way of knowing who understood what and, for all my father's research, he could not tell, when the wood came, whether it was really the wood the termites wouldn't eat or if he was fooled as well.

There's an element of trust involved in these sorts of things, he told me after the men left. But I didn't know if he was talking to me or talking to himself.

He was not finished for the day, though. He slapped sunscreen on his neck and did not rub it all the way in. Then he got out the boxes of pamphlets about diseases, the ones that talked about symptoms and how to prevent the diseases in the first place. They were filled with black and white sketches of people who were supposed to look like the people in Yuvut, and the words were written in a language that was a cousin to their language but not the same.

There was a temporary building for storing supplies already built near the hospital site. My father took the boxes there.

I went with him, wearing gumboots because the paths were boggy with the tracks of people and their pigs, and together we handed the pamphlets out. We went through one whole box on that first day, mainly pamphlets about dysentery and some on scabies. A girl who looked a little older than me, niece of the airstrip manager, helped us, too, acting as translator until my father and I learned through endless repetition all day the words for 'This is for you' and 'It's to keep away sickness.' Language school would have taken too long, Dad mumbled once.

The girl's name was Susumina. She pointed at me for mine.

Ruth, I said.

Ru, she said. The 'th' sound doesn't exist in Yuvut. Ru I became. Ru sounded like an older, smarter, more adventurous version of Ruth.

The people (all women) who took the pamphlets were polite. They thanked us as they took them. My father's face sweated in white beads as it mingled with the sunscreen; his chest rose proud under his shirt that he bought especially for the weather in Papua. High Performance, read the label on the back. Dad thought the thank-yous meant success.

Later I would find out that Susumina was an orphan. Or half of one, anyway. Her mother killed herself right after she was born on account of her father's new wife. The new wife was too young to feed Susumina, though she tried. So Susumina's grandmother carried her to the mission house that once was here. Her grandmother was the one who got pastel tins of milk powder and a pamphlet on infant hygiene even though she couldn't read. The tins were still in the grandmother's house. She kept peanuts in them, and salt. Painted yellow ducks scampered up their slippery sides, ducks nothing like the ducks wandering down the muddy village paths. In Yuvut the ducks were dirty white with red beaks that sometimes had sores.

Susumina was named for the tins, or rather what was in the tins. *Susumina*: *susu* meaning milk, borrowed from the Indonesian language, and *mina*, the village tack-on for girls that turned it into a name. This is how you knew all the orphan girls in Yuvut. They were all Susuminas.

When Dad and I returned to the house, we smelled onions frying in peanut oil and a chocolate pudding baking in the oven. Mum looked up as we came through the door.

I found enough wood out the back to get the stove going, she said. I'll make us a casserole. How does that sound?

Sounds great, Dad said, and he went to touch her hand, but maybe she didn't see him.

Oh, and I opened the box of wool my mother donated. I think I'll teach myself to knit. You'll need hats and sweaters for babies in the hospital, won't you?

Of course, said Dad. Even though it was too hot in Yuvut for babies to wear wool hats. He stood in the kitchen doorway for a moment, just looking at my mother, and his eyes crinkled at the corners like they always did when a join in one of his cabinets went together just right, or like on the nights when he and Mum put their anger and disagreements in a corner so they could watch TV together and share a packet of chocolate biscuits on the couch in the yellow house. Julia and I were not supposed to see.

# FIVE

*Dear Grandad,*
*So far I have counted eight different butterflies and there are lots of flowers, too. Most of them have sap that dribbles out and gives you rashes when you pick them. And ants. Chickens are everywhere all the time. They are all around our house and even down by the airstrip but the planes don't hit any of them. There are lots of people here that come and visit on our porch and talk to Mum and Dad. Mum says that they always want something. I think they just want to meet us. Some of the rabbits are pregnant, Dad says. Their tummies are fat and jiggle if they let you poke them. Most of the avocado trees have died already though. They got a fungus on their leaves that looks like white paint. I have a friend. She has a green skirt and a yellow shirt and a dad but no mum.*
*Love, Ruth*

In those first weeks, moment piled onto moment. The thank-yous did not last. No one read the pamphlets about sicknesses. Susumina's grandmother used them to start her cooking fire, and the woman who lived in the hut next door used hers to block a leak in the thatch of her roof. In my father's mind, the scabies mites still crawled over children's skin, dysentery still had its foothold, malaria was a thing that could possibly be banished by the sacrifice of a pig. AIDS was a mystery.

They're crooked books filled with crooked words, Susumina said of the pamphlets, holding out her arm, bending it at the elbow to show me. Our language is straight, we understand it. This language, we can get some of the meaning but not all of it. It comes out crooked.

We practised her language together every day, because I ached for a way to know how to speak about the new things around me. Susumina showed me books with her own language in them, ones that were not crooked because the letters walked their pages in the right ways so that the old women and men could read them, not just the young. She also showed me the markings etched on the shafts of longbow arrows. The words for these markings were the same as the words for writing. Her grandmother knew how to read the stories those markings told. They were not just arrows but books as good as any for carrying a voice from one moment to another, if only you knew how to read them. Susumina herself did not know how to read them — her grandmother sent her to school to learn to read other kinds of books, and Susumina had her life planned out: finish school, go to the coast, get selected for a famous football team. Preferably one in Barcelona like Ronaldo, but for girls like us.

Every day after lunch we went over to the mayor's house and sat outside to listen to the football reports on his radio. We were not the only girls there, though it was mainly boys. They pushed close for the best seats and sometimes they were so loud that we did not even know what was happening. All of us were there for one thing, though: Ronaldo, Ronaldo, Ronaldo. No one else mattered. The first time we sat and listened together Susumina grabbed my hand when our team scored a goal, like I might have once with Julia on days when she would let me. I almost pulled my hand back, but then let it stay. We pressed shoulder to shoulder, squatting in the dust, and the boys were happy and Susumina was happy and I, too, felt something that might be called happiness stir, and I did not know if this was a thing I should feel yet or again or ever.

I told Susumina about Julia when I had enough of Susumina's words to say so while we squatted by the airstrip, looking out for planes, chewing sugarcane and spitting the woody bits at our feet. Susumina and all the other children in Yuvut already knew what it was like to never see a sister or a brother again. It was not a strange or new feeling in this place. I told her about how it felt like there was a space now somewhere in my guts. Like something was taken away, and the empty walls of my stomach were painted with a kind of medicine to dull the pain because I was not ready for it yet.

It's your spleen, said Susumina. That's where you feel things.

Then Susumina took me to see the head pastor's dead baby. Julia was the first person I knew who died but I never saw her after that one last day at the hospital so she was not the first dead person I saw. Paula, wife of the head pastor, had a baby and it was a perfect baby except that the cord was twisted around its neck. It could have died before it was even born. It lay in its mother's lap as Susumina and I ducked our heads and entered the hut. It was a she and wore nothing but a thin white beanie.

I knew that dead things do not move, but I was still not expecting the stillness of that baby, the stillness of a body that should be at least breathing. Its skin looked as if a thin film of ash from the fire in the middle of the hut had settled over its face and limbs. Its eyes were dense and dark. Another woman reached over and closed them. I wondered who did this for Julia, or if she was sleeping when it ended. I was at our grandparents' house, Grandad was letting me win at Snap, when the phone rang and I knew before it was picked up that it was the call we were waiting for. My parents must have been with Julia. I can't remember. Even by the moment Julia died it was like she was scrubbed clean from the world. Not like in Yuvut, where we who were alive could be close to the dead. Could see. Could touch.

Susumina told the women with Paula about Julia. They all nodded, all knowing. So many lost sisters, said Susumina. Here I was not different from anyone else. Here I did not need to worry about people bringing frozen meals to the door to say sorry and have my face squashed against the breasts of so many women who said they cared but maybe did not really know how to.

Where've you been? Mum asked when I got back. She hadn't left the house all day and was pacing, waiting for her first loaf of bread to rise. She sealed her flour in rows of rectangular plastic containers to keep out the weevils and humidity.

We went to see Paula's baby, I said.

Oh. Was it nice?

It's a girl, I said, and went to wash the dirt off my feet.

---

We became chicken owners. They were gifts from people who came to the house to greet Dad and ask Mum for Band-Aids and medicines because it was common knowledge that being foreign meant you had these things. Dad attempted at first to keep the chickens in a pen made with wire from under the house and four wooden stakes. But we soon discovered that the chickens in Yuvut could not be kept in by wire, and we let them wander like all the other village chickens did. Every evening they came back to our house and it was my job to throw the dried corn and leftovers out in wide arcs to feed them. At night we heard them gently rustling in a tree outside my window.

Who knew chickens roosted in trees? Dad said, and he looked at Mum, perhaps trying to make her laugh. She didn't laugh and carried on knitting sweaters that would probably be too warm for village babies to wear.

I never was good at knitting, she said, unravelling rows and redoing them again and again to try and make them perfect, but every time she tried she stitched a couple of rows and then missed some stitches, and gaps in the pattern grew like sinkholes caving in.

Dad and I tried to think where chickens might elsewhere roost in the wild and realised that trees really were the only logical explanation.

A cat turned up and slept in the roof above the woodshed where the washing machine was kept as well. Small and thin, like all the cats in Yuvut. But this one limped and the lower half of its front left foot was all bone, stripped of skin. I could see all the individual bones and how they fitted together. Mum thought it must have been caught in a trap at some point. I fed the cat leftovers just like the ones I fed the chickens, and it was not afraid of me. But it didn't like me either. It started following Mum around the house every day, its bad foot dragging behind. Mum ignored it except to go to the porch door and open it when it butted its head against the screen, wanting in. In bed at night I listened to the sound of many cats yowling somewhere, their cries cut away from their bodies as if there were hundreds of phantom cats out there slipping through the night. I hoped that, if my cat was one of them, she would return again the next morning and wait by the outside water tap, licking drops from the spout.

Her name is Elizabeth, I told Mum, and, forever afterwards, Elizabeth it was. Despite the foot, she bore the name with dignity.

My father's wood arrived even though we still did not know if it was the right wood, and he sat for hours every day peering at the hospital building plans. Won't be too hard, he said to me when he saw me watching. Just like a dollhouse, only bigger.

She's probably getting too old for dolls, said Mum.

Each night Dad prayed and we went to bed by the light of the kerosene lamp. The solar panels were on their way, and in the meantime we were very careful with the generator. Dad planned to install the solar panels as soon as they arrived.

He reminded us of this every day, saying they shouldn't be too hard to figure out. Mum stroked his back. Her fear (and, perhaps, mine) was less thick in the darkness. There was space for optimism and hope. She did not have to battle with the knitting needles because the lights weren't bright enough. Moths gathered in the corners. But, at the same time, I knew the smiles that didn't last long, the backstroking, were all just threads that made up the silk screen that kept everything together after Julia died.

If you had only . . .

If you hadn't . . .

Why didn't you . . . ?

These were the sentences I listened to through the walls in the yellow house after Julia died, the sentences that didn't seem to have endings.

Your father is a stormy-weather Christian, Mum said to me once. She laughed to herself then, but I didn't get the joke. For him all weather is stormy, the world is always falling apart, and he is always desperate to hold things together and save them.

What type of Christian are you? I asked.

A potluck one, I guess. One who wants your father to be happy.

Dad ticked Anglican on the census forms. My grandparents on Mum's side were Catholic (in name, anyway), but she always said she was not ready to be Catholic yet. Or anything else, for that matter. But Dad was the one who filled out the forms.

What type of Christian am I? I asked.

We'll have to see.

At Sunday school in New Zealand I learned capital-letter words like Sin, Repentance and Forgiveness. They were good words for singing and decorating with glitter on posters that made adults look pleased.

Forgiveness in Susumina's language was not just one word. She showed me in an orange-covered Gospel of Mark, translated. Forgiveness for her was divided up and spread around multiple words because its meaning was too big for just one. Maybe if I could have used Susumina's words in between Julia's burning and dying they would have been better than anything I did end up saying. Or maybe they would not have been better, but I still wanted the chance to try them.

To make all the badness and bad feelings against someone gone: those were Susumina's words for forgiveness. Poof. Never existed.

Slowly, slowly, like words on a page emerging one letter at a time and maybe not in a straight line, or like the words of one radio channel accidentally getting mixed up with another, I started to collect what I knew about Yuvut and Susumina in my head. And so we started to settle into a routine. One that we thought might keep repeating through our whole year in Yuvut. We started to know where things were in the drawers without pausing. We learned how to turn the taps off just right so they didn't drip and drive us crazy at night. Dad started preparing the wood for the hospital with a shiny electric planer, and its rhythmic noise every afternoon, its own mechanical wail over the thrum of the generator, started to build into our days like an old friend or at least a familiar neighbour. He marked off his progress in his ledgers, and Mum and I marked off the days on that calendar. We began to feel through our days in this place like people walking down a new hallway at night for the first time. We tried to feel everything. We thought we felt something we could already call healing, when maybe it really was just a first numbing, nerve damage, a distancing of space and time. We did not know that this was only the beginning.

Under my bed in the village house, attached to one of the legs, was a spider's nest, a cocoon of grey silk. Soon the baby spiders would hatch. Like those spiders hatching, everything that happened, all our tears and ragged hurts, could be seen under the threads we wrapped everything up with. They were waiting, beginning to move. About to break through.

## BETEL NUT
*Abepura, 2006*

*Betel nut is part of the red that paints Indonesian streets. It helps take us forward in time in this story because real histories do not sit obediently on straight timelines and sometimes you need to go forward in order to see more clearly backwards.*

*Betel nut grows from the areca palm and has spread its way throughout South and Southeast Asia over hundreds of years, staining one mouth after another. When I found that I was suddenly sixteen, visiting Papua again with my parents from our new home in Darwin, and worrying that sixteen was the only and final time you get to do things like smoke cigarettes, try drugs, leap from cliffs into blank water, I bought betel one day on the street and I met Elena for the first time (though it was not the first time I tried betel). This is one of her stories:*

Elena sells betel nut wrapped in individual triangle parcels with its leaf, a bit of lime. She sells it by the side of the road that goes into Abepura, the town halfway between Sentani and Jayapura. Abepura is also known as the place that has KFC. In front of the big red KFC sign the ladies sell sweet potato, bananas, kangkung they grew in the sewers. Chillies, a pineapple, sometimes loose cigarettes. And betel nut. Always, always betel nut. In Abepura the lines between class are drawn by where you sell and, perhaps, where you buy. Papuan woman? Sell by the road, legs folded under skirts, arm up to protect the face from dust. The small tokos, little stores made even tinier by a profusion of wares, are where the Indonesians from elsewhere set up shop. Dust still settles over everything. Chainsaw, buckets of nails, tipping boxes of noodles. Inside the mall where KFC is, it is clean and the tiles are white, even if sometimes the smells from a sewer or hints of mechanical grease tinge the air. Here children wear polo shirts. Their parents are businessmen or in government. Sometimes there are American missionaries, wanting to feed their children something to make them still be American. At Christmas time there are rows and rows of plastic Christmas trees, every colour from hot pink to fluorescent yellow.

*Elena sells betel nut during the day, until just after dark. Just like her mother sold betel nut. Then, after dark, she puts any betel nut left over under her bed in the building she shares with five other girls. Except one betel nut she keeps aside for herself. She washes the dust off her face and hands, and spits red into the bushes until another kind of customer comes along. This is the kind of work her mother also did. Elena loved and hated her mother. Said she would never sell betel nut and never sell her own body either. But here she is. Two years ago she went to one of the new family planning clinics that the government set up. They did something to her that they said meant she wouldn't be able to get pregnant for a year. But here it is, two years later, and neither Elena nor any of the other girls who went there have got pregnant since. Some of the girls are happy about this. Some of them have cried. Elena isn't sure if she is happy or sad. She chews betel nut and it turns things like hunger and rage into dull balls rattling around inside her that can be ignored.*

*Every night she chews betel nut and waits. Tonight a man stops after only an hour of her waiting. He is one of the men who drives trucks into the hills and brings away the shale and limestone carved off them. Slowly, slowly the hills are being worn to nubs. He, too, chews betel nut, and afterwards they lean against his truck and chew and spit, seeing how far they* can paint the road red. 'You know,' the man says, 'my friend says the betel can kill you. If you chew too hard it makes tumours grow out the side of your face and down your throat.'

'Do you believe that?' asks Elena.

'I don't know.' He laughs and she can see his face in the moonlight, one cheek packed with betel, and his lips painted red like he's ready to go on TV. They can see the billboard for KFC from here. Yesterday the old man's face on the board was spray-painted over with the words 'Free Papua'. Since then someone has answered with 'NO' painted in the same black.

'Bet they can't chew betel in KFC,' says Elena.

There once was a different man, a boy really. Gone now. There didn't seem to be the need to resist when he undressed Elena that first time (a first for both of them, perhaps). Elena almost expected a clap of thunder and disaster, but there was none. Only this: his mouth hard on hers, a draught from a window that made them both shiver, an unending universe (it seemed) of skin and, in the end, that dark reddening ache in corners once unknown.

## SIX

It was a day that looked clear and innocent, on an afternoon when Yuvut was quiet except for the cicadas and a government worker's pet cockatoo that had learned how to wolf-whistle from Sumatran contractors working on the road. The news came over the radio. In the hangar down by the airstrip the men crouching around the radio sucked their teeth and made sounds that anyone could tell were sympathy sounds. In our house my dad shook his head and said I Don't Believe It, over and over again. Mum said Why Am I Not Surprised, without a question mark at the end.

It was the same plane that had dropped us in Yuvut. This time it fell out of the sky. The same pilot, except he flew alone this time, carrying sheets and sheets of metal roofing up to somewhere in the highlands. There were gorges up there no wider than the wingspan of a plane. There were valleys where no one lived, places with rock walls so sheer that no one could get into them, let alone get out. Places where things could be hidden for centuries. That's the trick of Papua — it makes it easy for those of us from Elsewhere to forget that a canopy, a mountain, can hide families, animals, gardens, civilisations. It is what made it easy for the Japanese and Americans to call it Empty, the perfect (though sweaty and often lethal) war zone. It is why the miners came mid-century, saying there was no one to stop them, and then the loggers, then the farmers, and the roads, the people, people, people. But if you just stopped and stood for a while, listening, you might be able to hear the voices of all those other people and things that had been in its mountains and by its rivers long before any of this. But, then again, you might lose them as easily as that plane.

Papua's forest heart wanted the planes for outside food, for medicines, for tools, for evacuations (civil unrest, medical). Everyone knew the pilots, because the same ones came in and out week after week after week. Between four and seven planes landed each week (I counted, all the children counted), and each landing was an event that meant people came streaming down to the airstrip to watch the pilots, the cargo, the passengers. Our family watched, too. Or at least Dad and I did. It was always an event worth Dad laying aside his planer and saw for.

The planes brought in contractors from other parts of Indonesia to start shops, build roads, hydroelectric plants (that sometimes worked), schools. Those contractors sometimes brought their families and sometimes their families started other families. But the people who had always been in Yuvut did not always buy from the newcomers' shops, and the newcomers did not always buy from the people of Yuvut. The newcomers did not call themselves people from Yuvut either, even if they had been in Yuvut for years. There was a separate Indonesian church for the newcomers who spoke Indonesian and were Christian, and rumours of a mosque for the Indonesians who were not Christian. We were the only people who lived in Yuvut who were not Papuan and also not Indonesian. The planes also brought in (and out) health workers, teachers, politicians. But these never did stay long and they were almost never Papuan. The pilots themselves were Russian pilots, German pilots and Australian pilots. But the ones who stopped in Yuvut were mainly American. Once there was a woman pilot and she let the Yuvut girls, including me, touch her uniform. Not as good as the Governor's uniform, said Susumina's cousin. But a good start.

The dead pilot lay in the jungle for four days before a helicopter found a path through the fog, and it took another three to fly him back to his family waiting on the coast. When they carried the orange body bag out of the helicopter, his wife dropped to her knees and sang because maybe that's the only way her mouth could make the big wide pain sounds coming from her belly. She never got to see him for the last time because the jungle is not kind to dead bodies. After four days his body parts on the forest floor met a different sort of life. Shiny-backed beetles, moths with brown wings. Worms, perhaps. His bruises softened and swelled, split open like a mango rotting in the leaves where it fell. No one told me all this, except the four days part and how his wife sang. But it didn't stop me or anyone else from imagining and knowing, just like no one needed to tell me what Julia's skin looked like under her bandages either.

I lay on my bed where the air was so still and hot during the day, and I couldn't stop thinking about that plane. How it could look so light and then could turn into a roaring twist of metal in the space of a breath. How our own bodies and the bodies of planes could let us down.

Another pilot came into our house for coffee during a routine landing. Pilots could do that in Papua, and a pilot was usually the only chance for people from Elsewhere living in villages to speak English to someone other than their own family. I wondered if our accents were changing. The whole island of New Guinea is home to more bodies of crashed planes than any other region in the world, said the pilot. The jungle takes them and then closes up above them so it looks like nothing happened there at all. The mountains seem to rise up where they weren't before. The clouds descend in seconds. The wind funnels down ravines, the gorges narrow, the ground can swallow.

You'd think they'd do something about it, said my father.

Who's they? said Mum. We're all on our own out here.

I thought, But how can we be on our own with all these people around us? There are so many people.

I started remembering (or inventing) things about the dead pilot that I had forgotten. That he wore a gold watch. Let my dad ride shotgun. Gave everyone thumbs-ups all the time.

When we flew out of Sentani we flew over miles of swamps where the only thing that broke through the green was the fat brown snake of the Mamberamo River. It left curves of still water and small islands where it had changed its course over the years. When land finally started to rise up out of the swamp, then we were getting closer to Yuvut. The mountains were suddenly there: the island's jagged spine. Geological vertebrae, said Dad. Yuvut lay in a short, flat place somewhere in between them. Landslides and old riverbeds scarred the mountains all around.

DANGER: HAZARDOUS TERRAIN, said the plane's robot voice as we turned in to land. The pilot ignored it. DANGER, said the plane, and it kept on saying it until we landed.

Sometimes, when you are small, you don't always think about how you got from there to here. You are just there, and then you are here. But the plane-crash news made me think about the in-between parts and the mountains and clouds that pressed in above us. And how we could not run from Julia's death or any death even here.

In *The Swiss Family Robinson*, the father says to the mother: *The world is full of nice, ordinary little people who live in nice, ordinary little houses on the ground. But didn't you ever dream of a house up on a treetop?*

The mother says *No. Mostly I dream of having a house in New Guinea.*

I wondered if she got that dream and if it was what she expected. Or if the people of New Guinea actually wanted her there. And I wondered if the family's house, or the treetops, ever betrayed them.

Before I left New Zealand I was learning about plots in stories and how they might look like a mountain if you drew them out, and how stories usually finished once they got to the top of the mountain, their most exciting point, or soon after. I wondered if this, the plane crash, was supposed to be the Big Thing that happened during our time in Yuvut, the one that would either make us go home or make us healed, or if it was only the mountain in someone else's life, not in ours, because we were taking part in a different story. Now I know that it was probably the latter. But, all the same —

DANGER: HAZARDOUS TERRAIN. DANGER: YOU MIGHT NEVER LEAVE HERE. DANGER: YOU MIGHT LEAVE HERE. I was not sure which option was the scariest. The language of planes started to be the language of my sleep.

# SEVEN

*Dear Grandad,*
*This is what I learned about today. The Cessna 206 is one of the little planes that are used a lot in Irian Jaya. A Cessna 206 can fit six adults inside, including the pilot. It has fixed landing gear, which means that its wheels don't go up inside it when it flies. A Cessna 206 can land on an airstrip that is only 300 metres long. A PC-6 can land on a short airstrip, too, but it can't fit as much as the 206 inside. The belly of a Cessna 206 is called its pod. It attaches to the bottom of the plane, just like the little eggs I saw on the tummy of a big bug in my book.*
  *The pilots here like to fly the Cessna 206 because it is good for mountain flying and jungle flying. It was invented in the 1960s, which is a very long time ago. The plane is good for mountain flying and jungle flying because it has a nose*

wheel instead of a tail wheel, and its wings are attached up high. The plane is fatter than some other kinds of planes so it isn't as bumpy when it lands as it might be otherwise. It can fit all kinds of things inside. Huge sacks of peanuts, chickens, rice, net bags of sweet potatoes, taro, things to build houses. I saw a pig getting ready to be carried away in a plane one day this week. Its owners wrapped the leftover bits of a rice sack around part of it and tied it upside down to a long pole. They covered its eyes so it wouldn't be scared when it felt the wheels of the plane leave the ground. Even though it might still be scared anyway. I would be if I was put in the dark pod of the plane.

I saw a pilot check the fuel in his plane once. In the Cessna 206 the fuel is kept in its wings so that there is more room for passengers inside its body. Sometimes planes catch on fire. This can happen no matter where they are flown, not just here. The pilots say that the Cessna 206 does not burn as easily as some planes do, but still easier than some others. Especially if the wings get broken.

When you are inside a Cessna 206 you might be sitting in the back. If you are, then you might barely be able to see out of the window because you might be short and there might be lots of boxes and things around you. You have to put a belt on that has two straps over your shoulders and one at the waist with a big red knob that you pull when you want to get out, but not until the pilot lets you. There are sick bags in the back of the seats like in a regular big plane, and a big knife strapped to one of the doors in case you need to get out of your belt in a hurry. If you get to sit in the front, like dads get to do sometimes because they are bigger, then you might get to wear a helmet and hear all the things the pilot says even though the

*engine is really loud, and you also get to see all the controls with their lights and numbers. The outside of the plane is all metal and it is a kind of metal that makes the plane nice and light. Anyway that is what a pilot told me and that is all I know about the Cessna 206.*
*Love, Ruth*

# EIGHT

I used to wake up at night in the yellow house in New Zealand, an ache in my lower belly, the door open to the long, dark hallway that yawned into nothingness. The hallway had embossed wallpaper that I ran my fingers over to guide myself to the bathroom. I heard Julia breathe, and her face had impermanent edges that blurred with the dark.

Night in Yuvut taught me that there are shades of darkness, and that those nights in the yellow house were almost grey from the leftovers of artificial light compared with the nights in the village. When the generator turned off in Yuvut, and the kerosene lamps were out, I could imagine that I didn't have a body at all were it not for the pinch just below my belly button. I could be just a mind, floating around in the black. At those times even my father was in bed, abandoning his radio. I lay there for as long as possible, trying to tell the frogs that sang outside apart.

But eventually I had to get up and feel my way. No embossed wallpaper, just the uneven surface of the walls. They were built using sheets of thick bark, varnished over. (Just as good as triplex, says Dad, and it has lasted all these years so why bother replacing it.) In the daylight those walls had so many knots and lines from when they were trees that I could squint my eyes and imagine faces coming out at me.

The bathroom seemed too large. The flush too loud. I rushed back to bed, the darkness flooding after me, letting my feet touch the ground as little as possible. This house never seemed to settle, always shuddering, creaking, letting the outside (air, sounds, smells) in. There was a stain on the ceiling of my room that grew when it rained, changing from one creature to another. Though it was raining less and less just a couple of months after we first arrived. The dry season, said Dad, and he told Mum that it was a good thing because the hospital work would get done faster. Drought, said Susumina's grandmother. It's coming.

One bonus of the darkness was that I couldn't see the stain at all. But I still knew it was there, right over my bed.

---

It rained the night before Julia's first day of school. The orchards were drenched outside, and somehow I slept through the familiar belly pain and woke to soaked sheets inside. Soaked sheets turned into stinging skin as I showered off in the bathroom, too quick for the water to heat up, too slow for my parents not to notice. The water was so sharp at first that I could not tell whether it was cold or hot. The sheets were heavy as I hauled them from laundry to line. Mum tried to help me, but I said no. I wanted to at least maintain the illusion that I was the only one who knew.

Despite how we hurried along the gravel, despite not stopping to pick the stones out from under the straps of Julia's sandals (her blood stained the new leather), we were late for school. My head felt light and high, a kite that could spin into dizzy free-fall at any second.

There were two classrooms at that country school: ages five to eight in one, eight to twelve in another. I hovered on the verge of being put up to the second, but at this time Julia and I still shared.

You're late, girls, said Mrs Jane as we walked in, shaking her braids at us. Names?

Ruth Glass.

Julia Glass.

Yes, like windows and broken and conservatories, and for eyes and drinking.

There was chalk dust and more shaking of the braids. Bored children rocked on the back legs of their chairs, catching the table edge at the last second. Two girls, my age, started whispering behind their fingers to each other. Flies collected in a corner of the window behind our teacher. Here, the beginnings of my guilt were conceived. The words sprouted out of me like great choking weeds.

It's Julia's fault. (And I did believe that in that moment.) I continued — She was so nervous about her first day of school that she wet the bed.

A giggle ignited the front row. The older children in the back rolled their eyes. Julia stood still and stiff beside me.

No I didn't, she said. Just that.

Sit down and get out your writing books, said Mrs Jane.

I wanted it to end at that, for my lie to be forgotten, but already the whispers, *Julia Wettaaa*, were coiling their way around the room, as sinister as smoke. I tore a page of my writing book and scribbled *sorry* on it, thinking I might pass it down the row to Julia. But I did not. I folded it over and over until the paper was soft with folds.

---

Just like that, my blame put Julia on one side and all the rest of us on another. All she had to do was say no, I thought. Or get out of our way and avoid the pinches and shoves that come with being at the bottom of the heap. Worse were words, of course. But she didn't, and then came the time we went to the river.

It was autumn, a Monday, and the ponds in the valley were starting to grow shards of ice around their edges. The weekend had been dark, cold and angry — to judge by chilblains and the restless rumbling shuffle of school children as lunch time approached with little chance of sunshine or fresh air. Luckily or unluckily, depending on whether you're looking forwards or backwards, the sodden clouds in the south held off long enough for us to be set loose for our one hour of freedom.

Perhaps it was the weather that was to blame for where we chose to run that day. Down we went through the back field, down below Mr Ashton's vineyard, to where the river bent and spread to a wide jade pool. Steep rock rose on the far side, but on our side the sand glittered. No one was supposed to visit here any more, but, as always is the case with forbidden places, many still did, including us children who knew that a stand of pine trees hid us from the road.

It was said that a female taniwha lived in the depths, down in a cave under the bank where an invisible current pulled swimmers right into her yawning mouth. Two boys from the high school had become caught in this current eleven years earlier. Their bodies were so pinned to the rockface by the force of the water that they could not be fished out for over a week, by which time the cave had spat them back out again to drift in the smooth shallows.

They must have been like giant pink raisins, Julia and I deduced. Experiments took place in many baths.

Six years after the stories of the deaths had been worn benign by the rub of constant warnings and retellings, children ventured here again to swim. The pool boasted a large population of eels, and it does not take much for a certain type of person to take the risk, no matter how little the reward. This time it was a younger boy who died, blond in some of the stories, red-haired in others. He slipped under silently and his disappearance was not noticed for an hour. His mother committed suicide that same year. We weren't supposed to know that, or about how she did it. She was hungry, we said of the taniwha, and she was a *she* because it was only boys who had died, and perhaps her hunger for them was fuelled as much by some kind of lust as it was by revenge on those who chased her here to this pool with their farms, their bridges, their white picket fences.

The pool may have been left for a few more years but for Arthur, a nine-year-old held back a year, who bragged on a Friday that he had himself swum down to the cave the past summer and survived, though he had seen the marks left on the rock by the desperate fingernails of those who had come before. Wreaths of half-moons. We didn't believe him, but that didn't matter. His story was all the excuse we needed.

Sunlight, grey and feeble as it was that day, had weakened what ice there was on the pool to almost mush except for a few large stubborn splinters that spun out from the shore in a whorl, an inside-out web with a dark centre. I sat on a log, breathing warmth onto my fingers, and watched two girls write four-letter words with twigs in the gravel. *Shit*, *Fuck*, *Slut*, *DYKE*, *C--t*. The latter with the dashes because even they knew better than to set some words loose. They shaped their letters with elaborate curled ends, perfect slanted penmanship.

Then I noticed that Julia had come with us.

*No* and *Fuck* and *Stupid*. These words I heard echo inside me, ricocheting as if against the walls of a sinking submarine. I imagined hands pressing to find air inside my chest. She crouched by the water's edge, skirt hitched around her knees, fingers purpled, cheeks white. What was she looking at? Mushroom, moss, stone?

It didn't take long for the other children to get bored, and then they spotted Julia. I watched from Mr Ashton's electric fence as first one, then another stood behind her, nudging her forward to the water. Then they fell back, acted like she was free, like the fact of her smallness, her age, flitted across their minds. Just for a moment. A certain trust in her eyes teetered.

But then there were three, four, five and more. All in a line. All those blue uniforms. I remember no faces. Were there voices? I can't be sure. My own was especially absent. When Julia was in ankle-deep, she went as though to laugh, half smile. Like — yes, this is funny, now leave me space on the shore again, let me lay out my socks to dry. But then the children were skipping stones and they weren't skipping them out across the wide water. The stones didn't make much sound when they hit her, only when they fell into the pool. The splashes were playful if I shut my eyes.

At the sight of blood, half the group became enraged but the others sobered. It was this latter half who slowed their hail and patter, and, after a few moments, the rest followed, the wave of their fury gone. Voices were heard again.

Julia found her footing on the shore. Some of the girls, who seconds before had searched for the perfect stone to hurl, suddenly found handkerchiefs in their pockets, and Julia let them dab at her forehead. Little mothers in stained skirts, their transformation was so easy.

Sometimes I believed that the taniwha slipped into my suitcase when we left New Zealand. She was the green of the centrefold of a fern frond, the green of pounamu, the greenstone. And it was possible to find that same green in Yuvut. Everywhere not regularly trodden grew thick with ferns in this place, and when we flew in on the plane I could see that where the river ran thickest, in its bends, it was like greenstone turned liquid.

I wanted to go to that river from the moment we landed, even if it was not a want I could spell out in so many words. I began to feel that even in Yuvut I might never be able to escape either the taniwha or Julia.

## PANDANUS
### *Nabire, 1920*

*The fruit of* Pandanus conoideus *is called buah merah, or 'red fruit', by the Indonesians, tawi by many Papuans, and it can grow to over a metre long. It is indigenous to the island of New Guinea and is the colour of sunset right when the sun is at its reddest and about to disappear behind the arc of the ocean. It is also an ancient fruit; its size is perhaps a leftover from when it used to be favoured by dinosaurs instead of humans.*

*Abok has traded pandanus oil with the Indonesian sailors and fishermen who come as far as his coast ever since he was a boy and first learned how to get the oil out of the fruit. Tumours, arthritis, worms, paralysis, skin diseases. These are all things the oil is said to cure. Abok was born with a bloody eyeball, according to his older sister who raised him after their mother died during the birth of a younger sibling. His grandmother put three drops of pandanus oil into his eyes and the red of it washed away the red of the blood until the eyeball was as white as it should be again. Just like Jesus' blood washes away sin's blood, say the Dutch priests who live by the wharves.*

*Abok doesn't know if either of those blood stories is true. But he knows how to choose the best fruits to extract the oil, and he can make a paste from the steeped leaves in his sleep. Sometimes the people he trades with come to him as he is waiting on the shore, but other times he balances small bottles of oil, layers of red and yellow separating from each other, and takes them out in his small outrigger to where traders have dropped anchor in the deeper waters. He likes this way best because then he can get close to the bigger boats to examine their wood and steel and think about where they have come from and where they are going next. His own father used to work on boats like these. He came back twice and brought Abok and his sisters sugarcane candy and clothing painted with bird designs. He does not come back any more but Abok can still use the pandanus oil to trade for cloth, steel axes and knives, sometimes cowrie.*

*His language is a mix of his grandmother's language and the traders' languages now. He has heard stories about Dutch ships on the other side of New Guinea, near Australia, where men like him can become rich by harvesting pearl shell that will be taken all over the world. India, Germany, the USA. Abok has thought about doing this. But he prefers to let his pandanus oil do the travelling for him. One bottle might go to China, to anoint an old woman's joints. Another might go down in the gut of a Siamese princess infested with parasites. Still another might get painted onto the chapped skin of an indentured servant travelling from South Asia to the plantations of Fiji. (We found a bottle of the same kind of oil in the back of the pantry in the Yuvut house, label sloughing off and the sediment in the bottom of the bottle thick like blood clots, connecting us and the house to different times and places and people we might never know about.)*

*After making his trades out on the ocean, Abok turns his canoe around and heads for home as the sun's light is replaced by the phosphorescence of sea creatures rising up out of the depths. Abok uses an old tin he found on the beach to bail the ever-present trickle of water around his feet, and pretends that the waves are starlight bearing him and his bottles of oil wherever he may please.*

# NINE

We could hear the sound of my dad's tools as he prepared materials for the hospital as far away as the airstrip, where the policemen liked to sit and wait all day, every day. The government in Jakarta sent policemen to Yuvut, long before we arrived there because there were stories about how the villagers plotted freedom from the Indonesians in their huts, how they did things the government called terrorism. At first I thought the policemen must be from Yuvut too. But over time I saw that none of the policemen sent for anti-terrorism reasons were from there.

Susumina and her friends called them and other people from other Indonesian islands 'straight-hairs' because their hair was straight, while Yuvut and other Papuan people had curly hair. Some (not all) of the straight-haired Indonesians called the Papuans things, too — things that were nasty and about the darkness of Papuan skins against the lighter Indonesian skins.

We are not Indonesian, said Susumina when I asked her about this. And I tugged at my own hair, in between curly and straight, and squirmed in my own lighter skin.

The policemen carried AK-47s and M16s by their sides, and I knew they were AK-47s and M16s because they told me and the other children about them as we crouched in the grass and watched them play cards. My one, it's been to Afghanistan, said a man who wrapped a strip of cloth around his head to keep the sweat out of his eyes.

Liar, said another. Look at mine. Killed ten.

The policemen liked to sit by the airstrip and drink Coca-Cola, smoke the cigarettes they kept in the pockets of their pants, carefully counted to make sure none were ever missing. Some of them brought glue for the teenage boys to sniff. When the boys got stupid, it made the policemen laugh.

They taught us football on the airstrip, because the planes needed it only those four or six times a week. The rest of the time the airstrip was for playing, for old women walking, for young men showing off with volleyballs in front of young women, for the policemen and their lounging on boxes of waiting cargo in the shade as the wind ruffled the unmown grass near the borders of the strip. The 'us' who played football was Susumina, some of her relatives and other kids who lived nearby, and myself. Two of the policemen played goalie and the others were coaches. They did not put their guns down for this so they swung heavy against their hips when they ran. The policemen did not run often, though. They lined us up and got us to take turns kicking balls into the goal, which was two empty paint cans and a piece of green string between them. There was just one goal, and when we divided into teams one side got to wear the policemen's hats that were usually damp with sweat. Mum said we shouldn't, that we could catch things. Things like nits. But we liked it, the guns, the hats; they made us feel like we were part of something important.

Sometimes the policemen grabbed the top of my leg and it felt bad, but I didn't know if anything like this was talked about in the Bible or anywhere else.

What do you talk about to those people all day? Mum asked once.

Nothing really.

Doesn't make sense to me, she said. Don't stay out too long. She went back to her dishes.

The policemen liked to take photos of and with me. They told me it was for their girlfriends or their little daughters back home. They had other pictures in their pockets, too — ladies with no clothes on, or just underwear, looking like they were trapped in the picture. Sometimes the policemen put their sunglasses on me and we posed; they told me to make a peace sign or let me hold one of their guns. Sometimes I liked this part. They held their heads next to mine and their hair smelled like corn oil and those cigarettes. Again, I was not sure what the Bible said about things like getting photos taken of you. The ladies at Sunday school back in New Zealand always talked about listening to our consciences to know if something was good or bad. Sometimes the photos were fun and we were silly, and other times I did not want photos taken and it did not feel good, but I did not know why, and the policemen held me so close on their laps that their sweat marked my clothes. The Bible seemed much clearer on things like murder and lies.

There were moments when I wanted to shout about these things, shout at my mother and ask her. I remembered a moment at breakfast in the week when Julia died — me on one side of the table, my mother on the other. Both of us screaming, my dad just standing in there looking at us. I do not remember our words or what we were fighting about. Only the roaring fog in my head, the pressure in my chest, the look in Miriam's eyes that said she did not know what to do any more than I did, and I hated her for it and I dared her to leave us, all of us, right then.

In Yuvut I stole an empty peanut-butter jar out of the rubbish bin and hid it behind the laundry shed. I got it out when I want to shout and yell my words into it, holding the opening tight against my face, the whole thing swallowing my mouth, and my words sounded like someone shouting underwater. Then I screwed the cap back on and put it behind the shed for the next time I needed to shout.

Sometimes the policemen pinched my cheek for luck when they were done with me. Sometimes I got bruises.

The first thing the policemen asked my dad every time they saw him, as they sat around smoking and looking at pictures of naked ladies behind their hands, was: You American? And, straight afterwards: You CIA?

My father always said no, and they always laughed like it was the funniest thing in the world. Then they shook his hand and offered him cigarettes. He said no again and left. He kept on sanding and cutting those boards. They were piling up at the hospital site, and every night he had to cover them with a tarpaulin to protect them from dampness and insects and maybe even people.

How's the hospital coming? Mum asked, most nights.

Fine, said Dad. Just fine. And he might show her the plans again.

One day I saw my father moving our important documents (passports, birth certificates, insurance papers, vaccination records) in their fireproof box from their place in the hall cupboard.

Where are you going to put them? I asked.

It's better if just I know, he said.

In the middle of that night he turned on our other radio, not the two-way one but the transistor one that you could sometimes hear Australian news on if you held it just right. He listened for hours, and I listened, too, with my head leaned against the wall between my bedroom and the dining room. This was just the first of many nights like this. Most often the only things we heard were sports games in countries I couldn't find on a map. Sometimes he found the news from somewhere like India, America, Egypt. I learned more about an earthquake in Italy and a massacre in Algeria than anything happening between our own mountains. The sound came in a rhythm, fading in and out, with more static than words. Sometimes my father made notes on a notepad, thinking he heard words in the broadcast that I couldn't hear. Or he thought he could hear the voices of pilots calling to each other high above the earth.

Did you know, he said, that the island of New Guinea has claimed more planes through crashes than anywhere else in the world? And most of them are never found?

We know, said Mum. That pilot told us.

In my dreams I saw the bodies of planes, piled high throughout the jungle. They were as soft and as crumpled as un-ironed fabric.

Come to bed, I heard my mother say through the wall. But the radio static wouldn't stop for hours.

After a week of this, I started getting up when I heard the radio switch on. I'll make us Milos, I said, and got hot water from the kettle on the back of the wood stove. The wood stove burned all day when my mother made bread, and the coals only lost their heat hours after she stopped adding wood, so the water was always still hot.

Thanks, poppet, Dad said when I brought him his mug, in the same way he did when I brought him cups of tea as he listened and pleaded with Julia's doctors during those three days of tubes and whiteness, my mother looking on and not saying anything, just twisting and twisting the strap of her handbag. After I finished my drink I went to bed to the sound of warped voices as my father twisted the radio controls and the antenna to try to hear them more clearly. In the morning his mug was still on the table, full. I poured the cold Milo into a saucer for the cat on the porch.

When we lived in the yellow house, my father used to watch the news on TV every night at six o'clock. Now in Yuvut, in addition to his late-night listenings, he started trying to hear the news on the radio at exactly six every evening. I wondered if he remembered that six o'clock in Yuvut is not connected with six o'clock in Nelson. That if our clocks didn't match up, maybe nothing else from there would match either.

You're not going to hear anything, said Mum. And it's time to eat. Turn it off.

You're probably right, said Dad. But he didn't turn the radio off and Mum did not ask him to again.

The people in Yuvut knew how to be afraid and not trust anyone, Susumina told me. From a long time ago, when the Indonesian Army first came, the villagers had memories sunk inside them, in between the ulcers in their stomachs and the malaria in their livers. Memories of arrows against guns. Memories of huts burning quick as grass, families nailed inside.

They had stories of airstrip massacres. There was a drought in other parts of the island that was on its way towards us, and wiping out people's food and water along with it. The people of Yuvut had heard from other villagers, whom the government called terrorists as well, or 'rebel insurgents', that army helicopters painted with the Red Cross came because there was no food. When the villagers, mostly women and children, went out to receive the rice rations they thought the helicopter carried, the soldiers opened fire. Because they never were the Red Cross. So, I did not blame my father for his late nights with the radio. All he was doing was borrowing someone else's fear and spreading its seeds as well. In Yuvut you could try to guess who was on whose side, but there seemed to be too many sides and no one was ever on yours.

One of the policeman goalies, Petero, always pretended that we hit him in between the legs with the ball. He held himself there, threw back his head, threw back his eyes. *Aduh!* he gasped. *Aduh!* One day we actually did hit him there and this time he was different, down on his knees and groaning. He got one of the younger boys to hold a cold Coke to his crotch. It left a wet patch that spread. At the end of the game, we ran away laughing. We ran like the policemen were nipping at our heels. We were so full of disgust, so full of delight.

We spent the rest of the day hiding from the policemen and shooting at lorikeets with our slingshots. We hit three that fell in streaks of colour. *Aduh!* we screamed. We arranged our prizes in a row on their backs, wings neatly folded over breastbones. I was almost sorry. Susumina would make their feathers into necklaces and sell them at the market with her grandmother.

There was a machine at a supermarket in my past life (a life that seemed too scrubbed clean in Yuvut). A machine with an iron hand that you could move up and down with a joystick to grab a soft toy inside the plexiglass box. With nowhere to run and hide, the toys just had to lie there and wait to see if they were the chosen one, if they were the one that bad things happened to.

## TEN

How do the seeds get inside the apples? I asked my grandfather when I was five, standing under an apple tree, he on a ladder handing down one heavy fruit after the next. All splashed white by the blackbirds that fed on the top branches where we couldn't reach.

The Tinies sneak them in at midnight, poppet. When we are sleeping in bed.

The Tinies?

Little people, fairies that hide in between leaves, rocks, roots. They don't live just anywhere. Only where they feel safe, and where there is a hint of a good story in the air.

He tugged on my ponytail, made the ribbon unravel, and we carried the apples back to the house. I knew he didn't expect me to believe what he said, but I wanted to anyway. His nails were always split and had dirt under them. He smelled like dry grass and Arnott's cream crackers. Sitting in his lap to read books or watch the weatherman on TV made me feel like I could never do anything wrong that would make my grandad stop loving me.

After the day at the river, I told Julia about the Tinies, perhaps as a kind of asking for forgiveness. They live in between the cracks in the rocks, I told her. And deep within the prickled hearts of the flax bushes.

A slow nod, a reach to stroke the clover under our feet. Green hearts between our toes. Somehow this drove the guilt even deeper, made me even more desperate to *please make her believe.*

They live naked, I said. Like I think the angels do, and Adam and Eve before they knew any different. They make the rooms and stairways of their homes in the stems of plants, in the cells, just like the cells we read about in school. Remember the diagrams I drew? I asked her. The orange poppy I found growing in a tuft of grass under the house? Its petals were creased like paper.

These are the words my grandfather taught me for giving the parts of plants their names, making them exist: stigma, filament, ovary. The way these words could mean something else or a different picture at a different time, attached to a different thing or body — remember that, Julia? How finding out which meaning is right is part of the hunt, the game, the coded story?

*Dear Grandad,*
*Did you know that there are Tinies here in Yuvut, too? They live especially down by the creek where I go with Susumina. There are lots of pools there where they can go fishing and not get swept away. There are also lots of places they can hide in,*

*like the purple cones of the sweet potato flowers. Those sweet potato flowers are everywhere, not just in gardens like you might think they would be. Did you know that flowers can grow everywhere if you let them, not just in gardens?*

*I think there must be Tinies living down by the big river, too, but I haven't gone down there yet. Mum thinks she or Dad will have to go with me because the river is much bigger and faster than the creek. I wonder if it is like the river back home.*

*I miss you and Grandma. I hope your apples are okay.*
*Love, Ruth*

Before she died, I made other acts of penance to Julia for not stopping the stones, not saying a word. Didn't put butter on my potatoes, ate more peas than meat, wore the hair-clip with the ugly flower that we both hated, didn't let the tap water run hot. It didn't occur to me to wonder if Julia knew whether I was doing this for her, or why, if she did know, she should care. Instead, I left dried buttercups on her pillow and imagined whole conversations in which I was the one wronged and filled with indignation, and in which she thanked me and we were both healed. It was enough to make me cry righteous tears into my pillow at night.

I found a velvet brooch with a silver back under the swing set on the playground. Or I may have stolen it from another child. I forget which version is the truth. I rubbed the dirt off the embroidery, trimmed its loose threads and carried it back to the pool where none of us had been since the day of the stones. The brooch spun high in the air when I threw it, and

I watched until I could no longer see its colour as it sank to where I guessed the entrance of the taniwha's cave was. There was a flash of metal. The last signal of a lost tramper.

---

You swore in your sleep again, said Julia, waking me for breakfast one day, a couple of weeks before the accident. Maybe I'll tell Mum.

Shut up, I said.

# ELEVEN

Susumina did flips on the airstrip and her dress flopped over her face. Susumina was not wearing any underpants. Did her grandmother know? I wondered what it felt like to do flips with no underpants on. Susumina's legs kicked in the rain. The clay stained our hemlines, toenails red.

I am going to tell you a story about a hornbill, Susumina said when I finally knew the right words to tell her about the one I saw in the city. It goes like this.

There were two small children, brothers. Their mother said to them, 'Stay in the pig yard.' So they did, while she went and cooked some sweet potato leaves. After that, a fierce man came into her hut and told her to come with him.

But she said, 'I can't, my children are waiting in the pig yard.'

Well he said, 'Come quickly, leave your children.'

And she said, 'My children . . .'

And he was forceful and said, 'No, come quickly,' and they went, leaving the children behind, and a small pig with them. They left and crossed many rivers and they went as far as Nanggerago, which is a place by another river between mountains that are different from ours. And that is where they lived. The woman became the man's wife and there were soon more children.

The two brothers waited in the pig yard for their mother and got covered in dirt. In the evening they got hungry and returned to their mother's hut, but their mother was not there. They said, 'Oh no, where has our mother gone?' and they searched and searched but could not find her. They said, 'The fierce man has taken her and left', and they cried as they slept.

After they slept and cried all night, a hornbill bird came. The hornbill asked, 'What is wrong with you?'

The brothers replied, 'A wild man has taken our mother away.'

When they said that, the hornbill told them to hang onto his wings. They hung on to his wings, and the hornbill carried the two small children far away until he put them down at the entrance to his home. He alone could raise them now, so he did. They grew up, he raised them, and when they became young men with hair on their faces ready to take wives he gave them smoothed spears, axes and strung bows.

At about this time there was a big event at the place where their mother had been taken. During the event, the hornbill sent his children who had become youths ahead as forerunners. He had armed them. While many people were singing, the hornbill, now in the shape of a man, started walking, leaning on a walking stick because he was old. The brothers went in ahead of him and they saw the man who had taken their mother.

The brothers had spears and fancy decorations. Using their spears they ran back and forth to meet the people at the event.

While they went back and forth they saw their mother.

The mother saw them, too, and thought, 'Those are my children!' As she thought this, she cried and she stared out to where they were. After they had finished singing and running, the young brothers looked at their mother and the man who took her.

'This is the woman, our mother, who was carried away,' they thought, and they found out where the man slept, where his house was. In the evening, in the darkness while the man and his wife slept, they quietly entered to kill them. And they cut up the man and speared him, and they killed their mother and her small children, her many small children that she had after she was taken. They just came and strangled them. As they killed their mother they said to her, 'You didn't care for us, you were taken away and you didn't think "Oh, my children," and for that we are killing you.'

Well, that's what they did, that's what the hornbill did and the brothers did from start to finish.

But what does it mean? I asked Susumina after she told the story. When the sons killed their mother there was a twinge in me somewhere, and I didn't know if it was a feeling of being pleased or of being afraid or horrified. Being horrified seemed like the right thing to feel.

Susumina looked at me and shrugged. Why does it matter? That's how it happened so that's how I tell it.

We went and sat in front of her grandmother's hut and chewed sugarcane until our teeth ached.

We played at being spirits down by the creek, because this world had creeks, too, but different from the cooler, clearer ones I used to know. Near the bank were pockets of mud that smelled like a bathroom and was good for painting faces and making dams.

We played good spirits, bad spirits, some spirits who were both. Spirits who changed themselves into birds of paradise when humans came looking. That was Susumina. Spirits who liked to hide by the water and catch dragonflies, touch plastic wings attached to even more plastic-like bodies. That was me. There are all kinds of birds of paradise, Susumina told me with her hands, with the flowers of a hibiscus plant, with leaves. Words had kept growing between us. Looking back, it feels like it happened without us even trying, but that is probably not true. It was like one day the world was only one language, could be talked of only in black and white, and the next all was colour because the extra words made it so. I had been given the gift of extra senses.

In Susumina's world (that was becoming partially my world, too) there were birds of paradise with bodies of ruby red. They stayed close to the ground. There were birds of paradise with yellow-cream tails that arched and bloomed over their backs. There were ones with tails in ribbons, with tails in wires, with tails that had spots pretending to be eyes. There were ones with ruffled collars, with ballerina skirts. Susumina could do their dance on the log bridge that crossed the creek. She could call for a friend and vanish into the trees.

While Susumina danced, I crouched in the water. Baby fish, thin and silver, darted under the roots of a half-submerged tree. There were mosquitoes that bit at the skin not covered by my clothes and I did not care. I was a water spirit. I was in the water. I was powerful and no one could reach through the daylight and touch me. There I was, surrounded by the sweet potato vines' purple trumpets because they loved the dampness of the earth near the creek. They were so purple, so full, I could almost believe sound came from their open mouths.

I said that my world went from black and white to coloured, but strangely, in this world where colours were so rich that fingers might be dipped in them, the language of Susumina had only three colour words: dark, light and red. But there were many more ways here to say certain actions than there could be in my own language. So my language gave Susumina other colours and hers gave me hundreds of ways to hit, hundreds of ways to betray, hundreds of ways to be a family, hundreds of ways to cry, to tell, to love someone, to know.

# FERN
*Yuvut, 2004*

*Botanical sources say that scientific knowledge regarding ferns in West Papua remains incomplete. Imperfect, unfinished, as if ferns are a thing that could be finished. They vary widely, from ground ferns such as* Angiopteris *to epiphytic* Davallia. *From the fine-leaved silvery ones that glow in moonlight and in the hair of Yuvut girls at play, to the wide-leaved and dark ones, cooked darker in the rock feast-pits underneath taro and the carcasses of pigs.*

*They came to the house for Mara's mother's best friend in the darkest time of night: that time right before dawn when the spirits of the island of New Guinea gather at the entrance of the tunnel where the sun is still hidden. This is the time when the spirits discuss the direction of the coming day: good or evil? Chaos or calm?*

*They came for Mendina, Mara's mother's best friend, because they called her a witch. Mendina wore a fake Adidas shirt that she bought because it had a cute boy on the front and it was comfortable for sleeping in. They didn't give her time to put on a skirt or shoes. Usually she wore a pleated skirt, deep plum, that Mara had grown up with, clutching its edges.*

*They called her a witch because Philemon who lived down by the river lost a baby boy that night and the old women said someone must have placed a curse on it. Someone else said that Mendina was seen walking by Philemon's house right around the time the baby got sick, so it must have been her who laid the curse.*

*They took Mendina to a clear patch of earth near the market, all ferny around its edges. They brought one of her pigs and cut its throat. If the pig died quickly, then Mendina was guilty. If it died slow, then she was innocent. Pigs and women were close in Mara's village. Women kept their pigs in their houses with them, kept them warm by the fire, carried them as piglets in the wide net bags that swung from their heads, even suckled them along with their own babies. The men who came for Mara's mother's best friend knew that the pig's death would tell them the truth. The lorikeets were just starting to wake up in the trees.*

*The pig died quickly.*

*Mara's mother jumped forward. Other women pulled her back. Many people had gathered. A machete is the most useful thing one can have in Papua. It clears grass from paths, chops fruit for a meal, kills snakes. When the pig died, Philemon gave a nod, and the people leapt forward with their machetes. There wasn't time for Mendina to call out.*

*Later Mara's mother gathered up some of the bloody dirt and wrapped it in stained fern fronds. Everything else left of her friend was taken away and thrown in the pits where rubbish was burned. For weeks afterwards Mara was afraid to breathe in deep in case she smelled Mendina on the wind.*

*Witch killings are not unheard of in Papua's mountains, and they are not unheard of in other places, though they might be called something different. She was someone who wasn't supposed to matter. A woman alone, and now a witch. She was someone who no one was supposed to miss. Mara's mother knew that the killings, which came in clusters like insects just discovering a newly dropped fruit, always started with the prostitutes, the rumoured prostitutes, then the unmarried mothers, then other women alone. Because these are the women who people think are the easiest to kill.*

*Now, when Mara thinks of the Papua that was, the one before Mendina's death and growing older changed things forever, this is what she remembers. It is the time in between darkness and morning light. She lifts the rusted latch on the small shop door where she and her mother sell and sleep, steps out onto the wet grass (barefoot in defiance of her mother's fear of hookworm and other parasites). She lies down on a plank of wood left out by one of her uncles who probably promised her mother he was going to fix something in the house with it, stretches her six-year-old spine against its splintered wood. The rooster they have locked up so they can eat it next Sunday scratches at the netting of its cage. A pink dawn lifts the mist from the trees, and birdsong starts with rainbow lorikeets flying dark against the new light. Mara imagines catching their bird voices in her hands until they overflow. The mist is laced with the smell of charred wood, rubbish from an open pit, yesterday's rain. This is the Papua Mara will not forget, but it is a Papua that is not hers any more. She is not sure whose it is becoming.*

## TWELVE

When a doll burns, its hair goes first. Then the padded cotton torso, if it is one of those porcelain dolls that used to be made that way. It curls and peels, like I now know skin will do. The eyes melt and turn black, plastic pupils relaxing backwards in the heat, and the porcelain doesn't really burn but glows red. Cracks, snaps. There are charred edges. In the end, all that is left are blackened porcelain toes, an empty porcelain skull. And porcelain fingers curled into permanent fists.

A week before the accident, Mum gave my old nightgown to Julia. It's too small for you, she said to me. There's no point keeping it if someone else can use it.

The nightgown was pale blue satin, with lace around the neck and cuffs, and one pink satin rosebud. There used to be more rosebuds, but I wasn't the first to have the nightgown either, and they had dropped off one by one.

It's a bit cheap and nasty, said Dad when I told him that Mum was making me give it to Julia. Why do you want to keep it anyway?

It's not fair, I said. How come something can be mine one day and then not the next?

Listen to your mum, said Dad.

Julia got the nightgown. It wasn't even night when she put it on. Plus it was autumn, and it was too thin for that time of year. But she pretended she wasn't cold.

I'm pretty, aren't I? said Julia to Dad as he went out the door towards his shed.

Very, he said, and Julia looked at me to make sure I had heard.

Julia had a doll called Eleanor In The Red Dress. She was part of Mum's old collection of porcelain dolls. Her mother used to say that if she kept them pretty and didn't play with them they might be worth something one day. A sort of miniature insurance policy.

If you get my nightgown then I get your doll, I said, walking towards our bedroom.

You can't do that, said Julia. Mum won't let you.

Is she not letting me now? I picked up Eleanor In The Red Dress by her hair and carried her outside and out to the orchard where someone, probably my grandfather, had left an old steel drum to rust. The time at the river, and how I owed Julia for that, chewed at the back of my brain. I ignored it and twisted the doll's hair harder.

What are you doing? said Julia, angry now, and reaching for it. But I tossed the doll into the drum and now neither of us could reach her because it was too deep. I could still get her out, I thought. With something that has a hook on the end, or a rake maybe.

But Julia was in the nightgown and the wind was sharp and dry, scaling our elbows pink. I had a green plastic lighter in my pocket that I had found by the road, and the container Dad used to hold the lawnmower fuel was right there. Julia kicked at the drum.

You can't do anything! she said.

The fuel was thick like maple syrup and the flames were almost pretty at first. Like fluttering pennants at some private celebration. Or like golden lilies, the same as the ones painted on my grandmother's china. Wreaths of lilies growing all around while the doll face stared through them, up to a sky stripped bare.

Julia screamed, but Mum heard her too late to save the doll. What the hell are you doing? she breathed out when she got to us.

I don't love you, I said. And it was a kind of epiphany when I realised that it was crueller to say those words than to accuse her of not loving me. This was my victory.

Even so, I cannot remember this moment without also remembering a moment that must have happened on another day — my mother's arms and an incomplete lullaby about God loving me, her loving me, and that being the way things should be. But soon nothing would be the way it should be any more.

Later on the day I burned the doll, I went back to the drum with a long stick and hunted for embers that still glowed briefly scarlet when the wind blew on them.

## THIRTEEN

How's the hospital coming? asked Mum.

Fine, just fine, said Dad. But he was not showing her the plans as much as he used to.

Mum started work on a new knitted baby's hat for the box that was already overflowing with unravelling, holey hats.

If you kept on following the creek in Yuvut, followed it around the burial hill, down the side of the airstrip, and then through some of the gardens down to the gorge (give it an hour, longer in the rain), you met the river I had first seen from the plane. Below the plateau the airstrip and our houses sat on, the river leapt between limestone walls that at some points almost touched.

The water here was all foam and white until it ran shallow over gravel in the places where people liked to fish. They caught the fish with wide-mouthed traps, once made out of palm fronds, later made out of wire and netting. They gutted the fish with small curved knives, and strung them in threes by their gills with a strip of soft but strong bark.

I stopped waiting for my parents' permission to go down to the river, an action that was easier than I thought it would be. When Susumina first took me there, a cool wind was blowing, carrying a distant mountain peak's chill. This made me remember when my father roused me early in the yellow house to catch eels on spring mornings. The orchards took on a different sort of quality at that time of day. As we walked down the rows, the branches were dark against a sky just starting to pink. Ice on the bark and new buds made the first light sparkle in droplets. I wore one of my father's old jackets; there were still wood shavings in its pockets, and my too-big boots rubbed my ankles, scented me rubber.

We filled buckets with the heavy black velvet of eels on those mornings down in the creek. My father had his tin smoker and he taught me how to smoke the flesh until it was coloured tobacco and flaked just right.

Taste the first bit, he said, and put a piece in my open mouth.

We crouched in the gravel, placing flakes of eel on our tongues, piling the tiny bones in a tower as we picked them out. The silence between us was the kind of perfect that was so delicate, so bubble-like with its thin surface of contentment that it might break at any moment. I pointed out to my father the rose and pearl bellies of rainbow trout where they hid under an overhang of the riverbank.

No trout, and different eels in Yuvut, though. The people in Yuvut knew what to do with the fish and the rapids. They knew the dangers of the quickening current and how to anchor themselves to the shore, how to predict when a flash flood was near, how to find the hatchlings (clear, so you could see their bones growing) that hid where the current eddied. There was a big tree that arched over one favourite fishing spot, and no one took the bark from that one or chopped it down. It was where the blue butterflies came from. No one knew exactly how or why, but everyone knew that early in the dry season they crawled out from a hole in the trunk and then you could spot the damp silk of a new butterfly's drying wings. These places didn't frighten anyone because at least some of their secrets were known.

Instead, fear threw its nets near the places in the river further away from the village, where the water spread, slowed and then went into a bend. The river's elbows, some called these places. Where the river ran straight and narrow it was good, but the bends, where the water seemed almost still, were taboo. Why? I asked Susumina, but she didn't know the answer. Why? we asked her grandmother.

Because the old men said so, she said. The old men told us to keep away. And we did. And we do.

Many people did have ideas about why they had to keep away, though, and they told stories told by cousins' husbands' fathers about what might happen if the bend was visited.

You'd disappear.

If you came back, you'd get sick and die. Your family would get sick and die.

If you caught fish there, anyone who ate it would get sick, too.

For generations your family would be cursed. Women wouldn't be able to have babies. Men wouldn't be able to find women to sleep with them.

A spirit would sit inside your ear and whisper until you killed yourself out of crazy.

There were other stories about giant lizards that hide in the underbrush further downriver, near the bends.

Have you seen them? I asked Susumina and her family.

No, but if you go to the next village, then they've seen them, they said. They can eat people right up, no bones even left.

I showed Susumina a picture of a dinosaur in one of my home-school books.

Yes, that's what they look like, she said.

Susumina's grandmother told us the story of the lost woman.

What happened to one woman, what she did in the past, is like this, she said. There were some Yuvut people who planned to go up to Pikinam — to my father's, my older siblings' and my mother's place there — from their village at Ndokle. From Ndokle, there they came. All the men there, they all came with their pigs and their wives and their children and their sweet potato. Because their things were heavy, at night time they slept by the *yeges* tree, down where the government school is now built.

Susumina's grandmother paused and pointed down to the school, making sure we were paying attention. We shifted in our squatting positions around the fire in her house, picking sweet potato out of their charred skins. Susumina's grandmother continued.

While most of them were sleeping outside, because there no house was built yet, a woman, whose name was Agobaga, got up and went from that place to a place called Welakni. She went to cut grass, the kind for thatching a roof. She got to Welakni, and at Welakni a young man cut the thatched grass and gave it to her. He said, 'We'll build it together.' Though Agobaga was intelligent, she went with the man. But the man was not a man.

He was a spirit. The spirit took her from Welakni, misleading her heart, and he took her alone to the forest, leaving the thatch behind.

He carried her as he wandered around in the mountains. She slept outside. After she slept, the spirit took her to his home and put his own food into her mouth to eat. Because of that, after she ate the spirit's food, she could not look at people's eyes or talk with people. She got fearful eyes and she became wild.

The people from Pikinam came after her, searching. Eventually they found her and encircled her. By encircling her they tried to make her whole. They tried to bring her back with them. But the spirit returned with other spirits and worked on her good heart with their hands so it became bad. And while her heart was bad, she died.

That is it, the story of how Agobaga got lost. If she had been afraid and tried to save herself, her body would not have got lost. If she had stayed with her family, she would not have got lost. Because in her heart she thought that she knew best and went with the spirit, later she got lost. Because she did not listen to the talk of her fathers and mothers and older brothers, she got lost. If she had listened, her body would not have got lost, that would have been good, and she would have stayed alive.

Susumina's grandmother pointed at us, stared at us hard. This story is now finished. Remember how the woman got lost. She pointed at us again. We giggled.

After that, Susumina and I began to say to each other that we would go to a bend in the river, the one closest to the fishing spots but still a good walk away. We would meet each other there and we would catch a fish, gut it on the shores and roast it right there. We would set up a shelter and camp out all night and never be afraid. And then we would come back to Yuvut and everything would have changed, no matter if it was good change or bad change. If the stories were true, then we would be eaten by monsters or hunted by the spirits until we became spirits ourselves. No one would be able to bring us back whole, if we were even whole in the first place. If the stories were not true, then we would live and be strong and filled with the knowledge that we went to the bend in the river and lived, and this would help us through everything forever.

It became our mantra, our words to get us through everything. The river's elbow, the river's elbow, we chanted when someone yelled, someone threw a stone, someone somewhere cried, or was sick, or dying and dead (there is dying and the dead everywhere, but in some places you get closer to it). When I said those words I did not have to hold my breath whenever Mum asked Dad how the hospital was going. When I said those words I thought of that other bend in the river where Julia's eyebrow got cut and bruised, and wondered if the same rules in Yuvut might apply in other worlds after all, and if she was waiting for me at the bend with the taniwha and the dinosaurs. So perhaps I could get my forgiveness from Julia even though I was stuck in Yuvut between the mountains.

I taught Susumina and our other friends how to play duck-duck-goose; Julia's favourite game. Only in Yuvut it was dog-dog-pig. Calling people these animals was wrong in Yuvut, which is why we did it. It made us feel secret, invincible. Like other people didn't know everything about us.

Hide and seek became hide and hunt. We played in the bush behind the house, near the creek and along the airstrip, and even around the base of the burial hill where we were not supposed to go either. Yacob, Susumina's cousin who was much taller and sometimes faster than the rest of us, was usually the hunter. Susumina disappeared up the creek where the branches hung low. Ani, another cousin, chose to crouch between the stalks of corn that my father was trying to grow. I climbed a breadfruit tree and was so still that lorikeets gathered above me. But Yacob knew trees. He knew the breadfruit tree was the best spot. He stood below the tree, mimed pulling back an arrow and shooting.

Got me.

Yacob was fun and good at games. But whenever I played too long with Yacob and began to forget Susumina, she grabbed my arm and shook me until I listened. No, she said. You want to be my friend. And you know why? Because I can take you to the special places, the bad places. Only I can go with you to the bend in the river.

I laughed because we all knew that she liked playing with Yacob, too. But I wanted to believe it was different with her and me. When she held my arm like this, I felt like I had become Julia, the younger sister. As if there might be a chance that things could be rewritten, could be fixed. She would drag me back to our yard or the creek and we would suck the sweet juices out of a hibiscus flower or chase the chickens or find grasshoppers and make them live in old tin cans. Big sister, little sister, back in their places in the world. Knowing each other's smells and sounds and anger and happiness and wounds. If only we got to the bend in the river.

## FOURTEEN

But, most days, the hours were filled with things that made the river shrink back into the distance. Many hot afternoons, right after lunch, I sat with Sonya, the *pembantu* who helped my mother in the house. Sonya was young, maybe eighteen, but she didn't know her actual age.

I wasn't born for the killings on the airstrip, but I remember the time a mudslide took all the gardens near the river, she said when my father asked her. Mum did not want to hire her. Said it made her feel strange having someone else in her kitchen.

Ruth, can you tell Sonya to wash the sheets today? asked my mother every time it needed doing.

It's expected to have some help here if you can afford it, said Dad. And, besides, you need the help.

So Mum got Sonya to do the washing, the floors, the dusting of the ever-dusty shelves. And Sonya shelled the corn and I helped her, fed the rabbits, cut the vegetables for my mother to cook later at night. My mother did not trust her and hadn't learned enough words to build that trust yet. I was happy to be the go-between, because Sonya told stories and taught me how to peel the potatoes fast and was not afraid to slap me on the behind if I was clumsy or not clean. Not a hard slap, but enough to feel like someone (not me) was boss and had answers.

In the afternoon, when all the work was done, Sonya would search through my hair for nits. Nits grew fat in hair in Yuvut because of the humidity and the closeness of bodies. Some of the older teenagers greased their hair with pig fat because it was meant to keep the nits away. Sonya hadn't found any in my hair so far, but her fingers in my hair reminded me of my own fingers, and Julia's, in my mother's hair. Once a week, at night, Mum used to ask Julia and I to pull out the white hairs that were just starting to silver the parting in her hair. She lay on one of our beds on her stomach and we knelt on the mattress, hunting and giving each one we found to her to clutch until we were done. She complained about those white hairs, but I knew that all three of us needed those nights. In Yuvut sometimes the sun came through the kitchen window and showed the white that was thicker now in my mother's hair, but I did not ask if she wanted me to get them out. Without Julia it would have been a different kind of thing.

Sonya smelled like smoke from a cooking fire and corn from the cobs she had just finished shelling into a bucket. My father used to smell like new wood and varnish from the cabinets he once built for middle-class families in the city. In Yuvut he smelled like mud and kerosene. My mother smelled like clothes that had been in the back of the wardrobe too long.

Why don't you like her? I asked my mother.

I don't not like her. She's young. Too young.

Sonya had two children of her own already, both boys, and my mother guessed that she might be pregnant with another. But I was more interested in the too-bright colours she knitted into the bags she worked on in the afternoons, and the facts she knew about the different birds in the trees, and the way she could bounce a soccer ball on her head (even though she always yelled at me that she had no time for that), and the time I saw her sitting with other women after church and reading the Bible aloud so that even the old women who could not read could still understand. These things told me that I knew only a corner of Sonya's life — a fact that made me frustrated and relieved all at the same time. She did not need me or her job to be Sonya, to exist.

I didn't ask for her to be in my house, said Mum.

When Sonya was inside, my mother moved around her like they must never touch. But when Sonya had her fingers in my hair I sometimes forgot that she was not my mother. Sweat smell is the smell of a body lived in, a body that is solid and to which I could cling. I leaned against her knees until her eldest child came to walk home with her. I watched from the porch as they left. She sang the same songs to me as she did to her children and her nieces and nephews, but on some days I wanted those songs for only me.

There was an early winter morning at the yellow house, wood-fire smoke floating over frostbitten paddocks. Shuffling down the blurred light of the hallway in flannel pyjamas, bare feet on bare wood floor. Mum, just a quilted mound in my parents' bed, my father's side already empty. Lifting the covers (letting as little of the chill air in as possible), sliding in next to her, her hand tucking the blankets back down around us. And then my back against her unexpectedly soft stomach, her fingers rubbing through my hair, parting it, cupping the back of my skull, warmth like rivers over thin scalp-skin. It was as if her hand was the only thing that could bring me down and tie me back into myself like the ropes connecting a hot-air balloon to its basket. At times like these, I was whole and filled. And here I was, in a fraction of a corner of Sonya's life, feeling around for that same fullness again.

But this was Yuvut and Sonya had her boys and her old women and her bags, and my mother cared more about the bread than she cared about me. The bread became her special project. She only needed to bake one small loaf a day but she always baked two. We go through bread like fleas through skin, she said.

It was hard to bake bread in the wood stove. The stove was temperamental and liked to play with my mother's mind, provoke her, taunt her. One day it might burn the top crust, one day it might leave the centre raw. Every day my mother knelt at the small door where the wood got fed in; knelt as she slid in paper, then kindling, then finally the logs, praying to the sparks, speaking sweetly, coaxing. Her tone was as if she were talking to her best friend.

You know, you don't have to do that, said Dad. We've got the camp stove, too, and we can live without bread.

When they argued about the stove I knew it was more about Julia and the fire than the bread and the stove. He didn't think it was good for her to get so close. If she cared too much about one thing, then how could we protect her if she lost it?

This is how you made the bread by hand in Yuvut. You mixed flour, salt, baking powder in a bowl. Added a little sugar. Then you warmed milk with some of the hot water that my mother kept in a kettle on the stove. The kettle was always full. She added the yeast (brought from New Zealand and locked in a drawer when not in use) to the milk, and the smell as it bubbled was like Christmas, like the froth on one of my grandfather's beers. It's alive, said my mother, but she did not say how. This was all added to the dry mix and she used a spatula to fold in the liquid until it was as sticky as clay, as if she was making a sculpture just for me.

Then she kneaded. She kneaded on the laminated kitchen table that was small and shook all over with the movements of her arms. My mother grew muscles with this kneading. They were small and I thought about touching them and whether they would be hard.

The flour clouded over her shining dough ball when she sifted over extra to stop her fingers sticking. Then it was time for the ball to go into a bowl, covered with a tea towel, and it sat on a shelf by the stove, warm and humid with the steam from the kettle, for an hour before it rose like one of those puffball mushrooms I used to know about.

It got kneaded again after that, and then it was divided between two loaf tins to rise for the second and last time. How did my mother make their tops so smooth? Bare and vulnerable.

The last touch was to brush the top with egg. Only I hadn't found as many eggs under the house where the chickens liked to lay as I did at the beginning of our time in Yuvut, so as the year went on she started to use water instead. Then into the oven the loaves went and every five minutes my mother peered in the door with her silver torch, monitoring their progress. I imagined her whispering words of encouragement.

She often baked the bread in the evening, because the oven had to be burning then anyway so that we could eat dinner. She would be bent over one of her shining loaves when Dad came through the door after a day with his wood for the hospital. How's it going? she would ask.

Not bad, said Dad sometimes. But other times he said something like, Water got to some of the wood last night. Or termites. Or we're having trouble drying the cement for the floor because of the weather. Or the generator blew a fuse. Or. Or. Or.

I could see that Dad was working hard. He came back covered in sweat and grease and sawdust and generator fumes. I followed him when he was working sometimes. Sometimes I held his tools. My favourite was the level, because I liked to line up the bubble exactly, make everything right with the universe of straight timber. But I did not know how fast or slow hospitals were supposed to be built, so I never knew exactly what the right answer for my mother might be except the one that told her he was Done with a capital D. Done and we were going back home.

My mother often did not look up when he told her about the hospital, no matter what Dad said about it. Sometimes she kneaded the bread harder. My father's hospital wood might be eaten by termites, a neighbour's baby might die, tropical ulcers might bite into my shins, the water supply could dry up, her boxes of soap and toilet paper might run out. But the bread had to bake.

---

There was one woman I think my mother trusted in Yuvut. The old lady first visited my mother on the back porch the day after we arrived, and brought her eggs padded with sweet potato leaves in her skirt pockets. My mother tried to pay her but the old lady said no. After that she came once a week, sometimes bringing more eggs, sometimes beans with long strings, sometimes a watermelon the size of her torso slung in a woven string bag on her back that she hung from the top of her head. My father chopped those watermelons with a machete and made me eat outside so that the juice could bleed free down my shirt and drip onto the ground.

The old lady had a name, but we always called her the old lady because she was the oldest we had seen in Yuvut, and for my mother maybe she was the grandmother she never met. The old lady had no teeth. When she visited she sat on the bench on the porch, out where they could both breathe in the breeze, and held my mother's hands, and words poured out of her like those ants in the flowers that my mother kept trying to pick and arrange in vases. And my mother talked, too. They both talked in their own languages, but that didn't seem to matter and by the end of every visit both had tears. Whenever the old lady left, my mother stood on the porch looking out into the bush beyond the fence and clutched whatever she was given to her chest. When I watched her, I could not tell if she was happy or sad and I could not tell if what I felt was happiness or sadness either.

# SAGO
## *Aikwa River, 2011*

*Down by the banks of the Aikwa River there stood sago plantations waiting to be harvested and turned into* papeda, *the staple of the lowland people on Papua's southern coast. But the Aikwa River has turned brown-red and braided with the tailings of the gold and copper mine up above in the mountains. Logs, too, have slowed and thickened it. The fish died first. Then the sago palms browned along with the river. The people living beside the river retreated back into the trees, taking their sago with them. Every year the brown of the river gets wider with the leftovers of someone else's gold and copper and mud. Every year it chases the sago and the people further away. From up above you cannot see the people. Only the river's bloody wound, forever expanding into the forest as the trees try to hold onto their green.*

*Kuli's uncle, Tarius, remembered the explosions at the tailing pipes from when he was a boy. He remembered what happened afterwards, too. How the army came, and the people ran, and there were bodies in the dirt. In the mountain where the mine is there are bodies, too, from mudslides and collapsed waste dumps. At least, at least (Tarius used to say) their bodies are buried. They are covered from the light. On the golf courses, built for the mine's foreign workers, men wear crisp shirts and can retreat into air-conditioned rooms to drink imported beers.*

*Insufficient data, said the environmental impact studies. More research over time is needed to fully understand the effect of the mine and its tailings on the river and the landscapes around it. Incorrect data, said the mine's American owners from their Arizona offices as they filed their lawsuits. They published photos of smiling women holding their children against backgrounds of deep green, no scars.*

*Kuli and his mother now wait to get on a boat to Australia (where I will meet them, later). And this is why: Tarius couldn't forget the army and the mine, even though Kuli's mother tried to get him to stay still and work with his sago palms and come with them deeper and deeper into the forest where other people were going before them* and where they might be able to stay without pain for a year, two years, maybe, who knows.

Tarius could not stay still, his sago palms died, and on too many evenings Kuli found him out late with other men, crouched outside their church, sifting handfuls of river dirt through their hands until they were stained. 'Go home,' Tarius told Kuli. But Kuli watched them from the trees. One day the men did not crouch by the church. One day they were gone and a runner came, telling of the news. Of a car that caught fire, of bullets from unknown places. Tarius never came back, but a photo of him did.

The army split him open. They laid his bowels out in the sunshine for the flies and the ants to feed on. Dying can take a long time. The photo was of Tarius with the soldiers who killed him, when he was dead. The soldiers posed with him, smiling. The two who looked the youngest smiled like they were boys again, posing with pride over an animal they brought home to eat. There was no cruelty in their smiles, which is what Kuli remembered the most. Their smiles looked like the soldiers were about to see their mothers.

Kuli and his mother have already tried one boat, but it sank before it got too far into the shallow Arafura Sea. The sea, the river, both of which Kuli once thought were friendly, have turned cruel. They wait for another boat by the Aikwa river mouth, where it meets the sea, and they watch the river's darkness spread out into the night.

## FIFTEEN

Sonya and I made a loop of bright green rope. We spread it wide in the grass beneath a dying avocado tree and dropped dried corn in hills around it. I liked the sting and the burn in my knuckles where the kernels rubbed when I shelled that corn.

It was the rooster with the orange-gold head that walked into the loop, peck-peck-pecking. Tight we pulled the string, and he was caught hanging and flapping like a broken branch. Sonya handed me her red-handled knife. Its blade was stained pale green because earlier I was bored and she let me use it to chop at grass, seeing how close I could shear it at the roots. She then held the rooster up to me and spread the feathers on its neck, as gently as if it was a baby and she was running fingers through new hair. There was pimpled skin underneath the feathers, yellow-pink. It took me two slices. Sonya let the rooster go and it did a half-run, half-fall. Hissed through the rip in its throat. When it came to rest at the base of one of the pylons holding up the house, we caught it again and hung it from the branch of an avocado tree growing by the fence to let the blood drip. As I waited for the body to drain, I sat in the grass under the clothesline and thought of chickens and roosters and dark feathers that smelled like dust and dirty pillowcases.

The blood smelled like I imagined warts would smell if they had a smell. It wasn't until later when I was undressing that I realised I still had that smell in my nose, and then I saw how the blood had run down my wrists and pooled in patches under my blouse. I looked in the mirror and saw myself stained and I was pleased.

It was after I killed the chicken that my mother decided it was time to properly open the box of schoolbooks that had arrived for me on the airstrip one month earlier, along with melted chocolates and a game I was too old for, sent by my grandparents for a birthday long passed. I had already slipped out some of the books through boredom, but the guidebook and even *The Swiss Family Robinson* still held my attention more than chapter books with glittery covers and children preoccupied with things like ballet classes, pony rides, shopping malls and classmates. That all seemed so far away now, nothing like my present world. Mum set up a desk in the corner of the living room. Dad painted sheets of triplex with blackboard paint. He wanted them to be used one day in the hospital (for recording medicines and other things with numbers and long names). Mum cut the end off one and leaned it against the wall in our house.

I hate chalk, I said. It makes me itch.

You have to start school, my mother said. It was the only thing she seemed to know to say to any of my protests. She tried to do her hair well on school days, twisted it into a bun so tight that it must have hurt.

We did, eventually, come to a compromise: I worked in my schoolbooks five days a week until lunch time and then I was free to go. I think she felt guilty for this, as if she should make me study longer, but she needed the break, too. With me out of the house, and my father out working on the hospital site, she was free to sit on the sofa, read a book, without feeling she should be somewhere doing something.

But she tried to hide that she was trying to hide as well. She tried to do the things that made her feel like 'mother' in another place. Stand here, said Mum, and she pressed me against the kitchen door frame, balanced a cookbook on my head so she could pencil in a mark, just like she used to do every few months in the yellow house. But in Yuvut, without Julia's mark nipping at the heels of my own, trying to catch up, mine looked like it was a mistake, a random pencil mark on a white-painted door frame, meaning nothing at all. And, after all, even with the schoolbooks and the chalk and the pencil marks, she could not change the fact of the dead chicken.

*Dear Grandad,*
*How are you? Mum says that you don't always get my letters very fast and I also do not get your letters very fast. It is because New Zealand and Indonesia are very far away from*

each other. But did you know that other things travel in between New Zealand and Indonesia too? Things like milk powder and fruits and vegetables and even animals. It must take them a very long time. Thank you for the game and new underwear. I hope you are feeling better after your fall. Dad says you will be okay and be able to walk through the orchards again soon. I hope so. When you get this you might even be able to run! Maybe you can draw while you are in hospital though? Sometimes I draw, too. Susumina can draw better than I can. That is probably because she is older than me. I am not as good as you either, but maybe one day I will be. I am trying to draw all the plants and animals that I can see here that are also in the guidebook. See, it is very useful.

Dad built a new ladder the other day because the one he has is not strong enough. I heard that you are not allowed to climb ladders any more. That's okay — soon Dad will let me climb ladders because soon I will be old enough.

I miss you and Grandma.
Love, Ruth

# SIXTEEN

Despite interruptions like dead chickens, dead pilots and home school, the year wore on in Yuvut. On Sundays the voices of people singing in the church floated with the mist and grass clippings across the airstrip and into our house. At first, we just listened. On Sunday mornings hardly anyone looked through the fence at us. No one came for Band-Aids until after lunch. No planes landed on the airstrip; the police were nowhere to be seen; and the village radio, which lived with the giant scales for weighing boxes and peanuts and people in the tiny hangar down by the airstrip, was turned off.

My parents walked around the yard and held hands. It seemed to be the best day of the week to hold hands. My father did not work on the hospital on Sundays, so there was no reason to ask how the hospital was going. Dad showed Mum the mulberry bushes (perhaps brought here by some long-ago family just like us) that were trying to grow behind the shed where the generator was kept. I'll be able to make jam, my mother said, and we picked the few berries that were ripe and spat the stalks at the chickens. Mum sometimes did not even make bread on Sundays. She let my father make pancakes.

One Sunday, the voices started in the church like they did every week.

How about we check it out today? asked my father.

I looked at Mum. Dad had been talking about going to church in Yuvut for a few weeks, guilty that we had so far stayed away with language excuses, tiredness excuses. But after all (Dad said once), we're just here for the hospital and then we are done.

I think I'll stay back today, Mum said. But you might enjoy it, Ruth.

I wore a dress that I hadn't put on since a Sunday in New Zealand. It was starting to get tight around my arms. I let my mother brush my hair and pull it into uneven pigtails. Elizabeth the cat followed us down the path as far as the airstrip.

When we got to the church, children, smaller than me, were playing on the steps, ignoring the singing inside. Just outside the door was a pile of sweet potatoes, corn, all sorts of green leaves, taro. My father stopped to add some money to the pile. The offering, he said. His money looked out of place and lonely tucked between two sweet potatoes. I wondered if things ever got stolen from the pile, or if God was watching it too closely for that.

Inside the church, men sat on one side and women sat on the other. All on the floor, with their feet tucked under them. Children drifted from one side to the other. No one seemed to care what side they sat on for now.

A man stood up when he saw us, didn't let us sit on the floor, and led us to a bench that leaned against the back wall.

It's okay, my father tried to say, and he went to sit on the floor again, pulling my hand with his. But then more men were there, trying to show us to the back bench, shaking their heads hard when Dad motioned at the floor. So we sat on the bench. My father folded his hands in his lap like he didn't know what to do with them. The bench wasn't tall enough for his legs, and he looked like he was trying to sit in a child's chair. My legs dangled just above the floor. Susumina was not there this week. Sometimes she went to another church down by the bottom of the airstrip instead.

Some people at the back of the church watched us as the people at the front sang on. A boy blew his gum bigger than his face. Popped it. His brother elbowed him and pointed at my legs. Laughed. A woman on the other side of the church hefted her baby up on her chest so that she could twist around and get a better look. The baby had snot running into its mouth. Flies were mating, eating, dying on the window sills.

The songs that were sung were chants that seemed to come from deep inside the people's guts, somewhere below their belly buttons and above their waistbands. There didn't seem to be verses, choruses, melody. I liked this. It made it easier to join your voice in wherever there was a space. A man standing at the front called out, and everyone answered. The men were the deep hum that became the ground that the women's higher voices built on. The voice of the man at the front became the pinnacle of a mountain of voices, all clambering over each other to reach the top. I closed my eyes. I climbed with the voices.

Here it was easier to believe that once Jesus had a pulse. Ate food. Drank water. Had parents and brothers and sisters. Didn't know everything.

God, said the voices as they sang.

God.

God.

Listen to me.

God. Don't forget me.

When the singing stopped, the preaching began. It was hot in the church. Above us dangled streamers left over from some celebration, faded from what might have been pink to a dirty white. My father let me draw pictures in one of the little notebooks he kept in his pocket. His back left sweat patches on the wall when he leaned forward. There was the smell of the breath from many lungs. A woman crawled in on her hands and knees to hear the sermon. Her feet were twisted, too small, and dragged behind her.

Polio, Dad whispered in my ear. Too loud, I thought. The woman went up to the front of the church and the others there made way for her. She took someone's new baby from their lap and rocked it back and forth. The baby wore long sleeves, long pants, one of the hooded blankets that all the babies here seemed to wear. Looking at it made me sweat more.

And the sermon went on. We could still hear the children playing outside.

Can I go out? I asked. Everyone else seemed to go in and out as they pleased.

Wait a bit, said my father. But when another elder stood up to give community notices (someone's pigs were dying of a mysterious illness, a wedding for the pastor from another village was scheduled for next week), he nodded and I went.

The children outside had been drawing with sticks in the dirt but then found a pair of birdwing butterflies. I knew they were those butterflies from my grandfather's book. Their wings were deep green and black, and their bodies looked as if they were powdered sulphur-yellow. Two boys each held one, and then ripped off their wings and threw them away. They scattered like scraps of satin. The boys put the bodies on the ground where they squirmed and didn't look like caterpillars as I thought they would.

Hold one, one of the boys said to me. He put one of the butterfly bodies in my hand. Its legs tickled my palm. The boy snatched it back after a while, tossed it in the air with its mate, broke the bodies apart when they landed back in his hands. His hands glittered with wing dust, shone in the sunlight.

The voices in the church went on. I walked home without my father. As I came to the gate, I could just see the shape of my mother through the kitchen window, bending over the sink, rubbing dishes hard because I could see her shoulders shake. She tried every day in Yuvut to get the detergent to make fluffy suds like they used to do in the yellow house's sink, but the detergent barely foamed because my parents said the water was too hard, too many minerals. But when I put my hand into it, it seemed just like any other water to me.

Rose, my grandmother, used to come over to the yellow house after my parents took it over and after Julia and I were born, until the breaks between my parents became more obvious. Then Rose and Mum started speaking words to each other that were too polite, had edges that didn't used to be there. After that, Rose kept stones in small silk pouches for us instead, hidden in her lingerie drawer under neat rows of plain white underpants and thick-strapped bras. She showed them to us when we came over. Turquoise for Julia, tiger's eye for my mother. Iridescent moonstone for me, for femininity and balance (she said). Obsidian for herself. She liked to rub it between her fingers and will her anger into its blackness.

Seeing my mother in that moment through the window, before she saw me, made me think of my grandmother and those angry stones, how anger can be quiet sometimes, and of the ways that anger seemed to travel through people even when the person who started the anger was gone.

## SEVENTEEN

One night in the yellow house we heard the word Divorce.
    Wellington, my mother said.
    Too far, said my father. The girls?
    You're better for them than me. I'll visit.
    Please.

Then, after Julia died:
    Let's think about it.
    I have.
    For Ruth.
    One year.

Some nights:
 I love you. I do.

# EIGHTEEN

Every Monday, Wednesday and Saturday, the market, called the *pasar* in this world, ran down near the bottom of the airstrip. And every Monday, Wednesday, Saturday, my mother sent me to buy the things she needed. She never went down there herself, but before I went she filled up my water bottle, insisted on smearing sunscreen all over my neck. She waved at me from the kitchen window as I went out the gate and then let the curtain fall back in place.

The pasar had different parts. There was a tin roof built over a big square in the dirt where the tables were set up. This was where the noodles were sold, the eggs, the cigarettes, the lollipops and gum, the cooking oil, coloured string for the bags the Yuvut women made, nails that my father said were stolen, and (sometimes, just sometimes) party balloons, mainly red and orange.

There was also a special long table on one side where those who had meat to sell stood. There might be the body of a bandicoot split open, innards exposed, or there might be possums, skinned. Once a month or so there might be the leg or ribs of a pig spread out on banana leaves and packed with edible ferns, but my mother said this pig meat was too old or might be the kind with worms so we should stick to praying that fresh meat, with the blood still dripping, would come to our door to buy. Our freezer that ran on a blue flame fuelled by kerosene was stuffed with little packets of city-bought Australian mince that my mother rationed out, waiting for meat at our door to happen.

Some days there were eggs, not chicken ones, arranged beside the meat. Large and blue-grey, those were from a Victoria crowned pigeon; small and spotted, that was from a dove with no English name. Duck eggs, too, that we made omelettes with once, but they had tiny bodies in them trying to be ducklings, just two centimetres long.

Around the square of dirt, out from under the shelter of the roof, sat women in the grass with their skirts gathered up around their knees. They sold sweet potatoes and their leaves, taro, small purple onions, peanuts in their shells (still dangling from dirty roots), watermelon, bananas, papaya, chillies. These women also sold the small green betel nut that turned to bloody juice when you chewed it, the one that made you forget being hungry, numbed your mouth and all the way down your insides. Every Monday, Wednesday and Saturday I sat with Susumina and the women as they knitted their bags with their fingers, and let the waves of their talk wash over me. The women let us eat peanuts and betel nut with them. Orphan girls, one woman there every week called us. This village looked after its orphans.

We called the women our mothers, in an almost-joke. The ground was stained red with our spit.

Susumina and I held the balls of string for the women making the bags, and sometimes Susumina and the others talked about where they came from. My great-grandmother's people, Susumina told me, were the children of the pythons that live in trees. And my great-grandfather's ancestors were the adders that make you sick when they bite, but not sick enough to die if you are full-grown. If you are young, though, and the snakes bite your hands or feet, and the venom is carried to your heart, you die. And when the skins of those snakes touched, the beginnings of our ancestors began in their bodies. That is why we are forbidden to kill those snakes, because they are our relatives. We cannot eat them.

Susumina told me about the snakes many times. So I started to make up my own place to come from, my own relatives. My ancestors came from the rivers, from the pools where the eels live. That's why bad things happened after my father and I caught and ate some. That's why we don't live far from the water.

Susumina and the old women all nodded. That's what they did when I told them that I had a sister once, too. They all nodded. Everyone had lost a sister or a brother, a mother or a father or a child in Yuvut. They knew how it was.

The pasar was also where men liked to yell, where anyone who didn't mind being seen went so that announcements could be made, notices could be shared, news of the dead, dying and just born could be heard. Fights were fought and settled, not too much blood shed.

One woman stood up. Last week a young man asked her sister to go back to his village higher up in the mountains but she didn't like him. He beat his last wife and he would beat this one. The chief pastor and another elder stood up. The woman sat down. The pastor and the elder yelled back and forth with the young man until something was decided. The women sitting in the grass occasionally yelled in their direction. In Yuvut, because I did not yet know enough about people, it was hard to tell who was happy and who was not.

The pasar was where we chose sides. Even Susumina, the other children and I: we knew that we must pick sides. There were those whose relatives had always been in Yuvut, or at least always been in the highlands. There were those who were not from Yuvut but still called themselves Papuan. But, like the policemen were not from Yuvut, there were the children who came from the coast or from other Indonesian islands, the ones we called straight-haired, whose fathers worked on the hospital, in the school, in the new government offices that lined the top of the airstrip: they never did mean to stay in Yuvut. They liked to creep up behind us and pull our ears and hair; called me foreigner and the others dogs, scum, glue-sniffing terrorists or guerrillas who could never win. I had to choose, but I was not from Yuvut and my parents were not from Yuvut and we did not mean to stay in this village forever either. My hair was mostly straight even though I twisted it at night when it was wet. Susumina and Yacob and the ladies down by the pasar did not call me straight-hair, though. Even though I could run to my house with a door that locked away from the taunts when I wanted to, and even though we had the good seats in church and even though the pilots sometimes brought us treats from the coast or from overseas and even though we were going to leave one day. We all had to choose.

My mother had told me to buy noodles. And chillies, if I could find them, the long dark-red kind. I leaned back in the grass, dug the heels of my gumboots in the soft ground. Susumina got to bury her toes in it bare, but my mother scared me with photos of hookworms burrowing into my feet. If they stayed in your body long enough they could get into your lungs, make you cough and then emerge at night through the skin on your chest, leaving behind little red pin dots that you see in the morning.

Before I went back to the house I had to wash my mouth out so that my parents did not see my gums and teeth all red from the betel. I used the bottle my mother sent with me. She filled it with water she boiled and filtered because she said that other worms and worse things lived in water that was not treated like this. I washed and washed, swirled and spat. When I got home, handed my mother the noodles and chillies, sat down for lunch with both my parents, they did not say anything about any red. My father just fiddled with his radio, as usual, and my mother examined the crust of the bread. So I was relieved. But also, a part of me, a little disappointed.

## PAPAYA
*Transmigrant Camp, 2013*

*The papaya tree holds cures. For malaria, boil the leaves bitter, then drink their tea five times a day until the fever has left. For amoeba, crush the seeds, slippery like fish eyes, with garlic, and swallow. This will be bitter, too. These are the things that Arif has learned in the transmigrant camp on Papua's humid northern coast, where things like malaria and amoeba are expected and met like relatives no one loves but must entertain anyway. These are the lessons Arif will pass on to me one day in Darwin, Australia, as we both volunteer in the garden of a refugee centre and discuss things like plants because sometimes discussing plants is better than discussing other things at first. Diseases and plants are easier things to have in common.*

*Before the boat, Arif had a mother with a green silk dress and an older cousin who was like a brother and a father who wore crisp shirts to Friday prayers. Before the boat, Arif was not afraid of the sea as it tugged at his hair and pulled at his body with its currents. Arif helped his father most days of the week to bring in nets of silver and eyes. Every morning, when they went out in the still darkness, Arif trailed his hands in the water that was patched with light and shadows. His family lived together in a place that wasn't quite land, wasn't quite sea. Arif played among mangrove roots.*

*But Arif's father was killed by a man who said he did not pay his rent, and Arif's mother began leaning furniture against the door to keep the outside from coming in. She took Arif and his cousin to Dhaka, the capital of their country, where she might find work. She put the orphan cousin and Arif on a boat with a captain who said he would take them to Australia, along with all the others on his boat. Rust stained their palms and soles even before the boat left the harbour. This ends all the memories Arif has before the boat took them away from Dhaka, away from the mangroves, away from his mother with the green dress. Arif does not know where his cousin is any more, much less his mother.*

*He did not make it to Australia. He was told that he is now on the island of New Guinea, on the Indonesian half, in a camp for transmigrants from the other islands of Indonesia. The transmigrants were promised parcels of land in Papuan forests in exchange for land taken from their own islands. Some call themselves palm-oil refugees; some of them are here for the promise of gold, gas, timber, wide tracts of empty land. None of them are here to crouch under tin sheeting, watching the already swampy land become more bogged with the heavy rain. None of them are here for the mosquitoes.*

*Arif does not know how long he will be here. He does know that the mosquitoes here are just as large as they were in the mangroves in his past home. Sometimes he cleans latrines at the camp for money to buy noodles or a treat of betel. There are many single men here and sometimes he washes their clothes with the women. Sometimes he helps an old man with no sons sell medicines and other cures for everything from toe fungus (very common in the camp), to scabies, to tuberculosis. Sometimes he sees a glimpse of a green dress. Sometimes the old man needs to go far to get his medicine supplies and they push their way through the dark clay swamps to the beach in the early morning, where Arif is free to browse along the shore for tiny crabs and spiralled shells. He finds other things, too. Chip packets, cigarette butts, bottle caps. Sometimes scraps of clothing that he searches, wondering who they might have belonged to. He has a fever again, and the old man is going to start boiling the papaya leaves when they get back to camp.*

*Arif stands with his feet in the sea that used to be a friend and then was not and now is something that brings him gifts he does not know how to use. He sees the Morning Star up above, dawn's sky holding onto traces of the night. Mother, he wants to say to the waves, Mother, come find me in this place. Let the sea take me back.*

*Papaya is the answer to many sicknesses. Arif knows this. But he does not know if it will cure what he has.*

# NINETEEN

A man came and sat on our front porch, complaining to my father about the demon on his back.

You see it? he demanded. You see it?

He described it as a creature cut from brown leather, with hands that, despite their softness, were throttling him.

Here's some antibiotics, said my mother. I think you have a throat infection.

The man went away. Later, I saw him selling the antibiotics at the market. Two tablets for a fresh egg or a pack of gum, he told me.

Every night my father prayed and my mother counted the medicines in their locked box. How much longer do you need for the hospital? I heard. I did not always hear the answer but I heard the radio switching on and off, on and off.

# TWENTY

When I look back on that time now, was everything just building, building towards what happened next? Is that how things work in real life or do they only seem that way when we look at them from a distance? This is how I tell it now:

Then came the interruptions to our village life again. Bigger, this time, than a pilot falling out of the sky. Even I knew this. One day the little pink-red notes the women clutched at the pasar weren't worth gum or lollipops any more. The pilots told my father that the rupiah was dropping fast. A good time for people like us, they said. They meant, for people who can get money from elsewhere. Not so good for the people who got their money from Yuvut or in the rest of Indonesia, though. The women in Yuvut started clipping notes together in little piles, and they needed to pile those notes higher and higher every week to buy noodles, cooking oil, rubber bands for their hair.

When we first got to the village, everywhere — in the shed by the airstrip, in the places where the policemen slept, in the government shops, in some people's houses — there was President Suharto hanging on the wall, looking down over all of us. He was everywhere except for the market. No walls meant no nails to hang Suharto's face on. Maybe he couldn't watch us there.

Who's Suharto? I asked my father when we first arrived.

He's been the President for a long time. Killed lots of communists in the sixties. Don't talk about him to other people. He has ears and we have our visas to worry about.

And I remembered something from history books about having to hate the communists and their type of red but I could not remember why.

But then it was May 1998 and there were more planes landing on the airstrip, and sometimes there were soldiers who got out of those planes and stayed. And the pictures of Suharto came down. Another President went up. But people weren't so careful to have him in their houses. Now there were fewer eyes looking over our peanuts and bags of rice. My father heard stories from the American pilots and from his radios. I heard bits of them when I followed my father onto the airstrip when he went to say hello to the pilots. I crouched under the tail flaps of the plane and leaned against the still-warm body. The stories were of people rioting in the cities all across Indonesia. Rioting for many reasons. In Papua they rioted for independence and against poverty and hunger, against Suharto. Elsewhere in Indonesia they rioted against rapes, the military, economic instability, against Suharto, and some for Suharto. Turning over cars, flashing knives, kidnapping, setting things on fire. There were also stories of dead bodies, missing bodies, floating bodies. The soldiers and policemen shrugged and let my father and the pilots talk.

More planes came, planes that were too big for the airstrip and left long ruts so deep in the dirt we could roll tennis balls down them. These planes were not flown by Americans, and they brought bags of rice from the government to give to the people of Yuvut for free because money was not worth much any more and because the radio said drought, called El Niño, following a pattern called La Niña, had finally found his way to us. I drew El Niño and La Niña for a school assignment on the seasons. I made La Niña a woman with dark hair and wide skirts that whipped the world cold, and then, when she met El Niño, her skirts wrapped the world like cellophane, sealing us away from the rain clouds. A hot wind always blew around the feet of my couple and burnt off any cloud or fog as they formed.

My father found out that the pastors and headman of Yuvut started counting dead people and trees, adding those numbers to the numbers of live people in the village, and then writing them all down on the ration papers from the government so that they could get more rice.

Is it ethical not to let the police know this is going on? Mum asked him.

I don't know. It almost seems the opposite, that it would be unethical to tell the police. I mean, what else do they have?

The kind of rules you can break and the ones you can't were different in this place.

I'm too young to remember the first Suharto fighting, said Susumina's stepmother. But now I am here and remembering, and Suharto is gone but the angriness goes on.

Time was measured differently in Yuvut than it was in my past world. Susumina's grandfather said he was too young to remember when the Dutch explorers first came to the area and brought their metal tools, but at the time of the killings on the airstrip he was the new father of Susumina's aunt. The story was the same whenever you asked someone how old they were. They used things that happened to measure lives, not numbers on a line. Like the time when the first missionaries came up through the valley and made the measurements for the airstrip: If someone was a child and remembered that time, or even helped chop the trees or carry branches away from the spot for the airstrip, then this meant they were very old. Another good way to measure the length of a life in Yuvut was by the big killings. The big killings happened sometime in the seventies. When I was a young woman and had my first child, said Susumina's grandmother. Aben, Yacob's father, who waited for Dad by the fence to sell him wood and who taught him new words, said that he was a boy when it happened. Maybe a year before it was his turn to move from his mother's house into the men's house with his father.

It all started over a volleyball game. Or, at least, that's what it looked like at first. Some of the young men in Yuvut invited the Indonesian military officers to play. This was the time when the Indonesian military were quietly appearing throughout Papua's valleys with their guns. They were in Yuvut because they heard that some of Yuvut's men were OPM, or *Operasi Papua Merdeka*. Operation Papua Freedom. This name makes it sound like a spy thing or like Papua had its own army and this was their mission — to gain independence for Papua from Indonesia. But OPM and their mission were, and are, more like ghosts than anything else. More like shapes in the forests whose outlines you never quite see. More like stories than bodies, until one dies and is brought home to his family. More like a wish than a mission, because forests are hard to speak across and most of those young men who might have called, or still call, themselves OPM were just trying to connect all their voices together, or trying to believe that their voices could be connected and become more than just whispers in the dark.

On the day of this volleyball game, the sun was high. The game started, normal enough at first, except it was hard not to notice (so I was told) the differences in uniform. Some of the military men removed their shirts though. The military men brought their guns, as expected, and the Yuvut men, at least some of them, brought their machetes. Children played on the fringes of the game, imitating the older men, making faces behind an uncle's or a soldier's back.

Some said that the trouble began over a disagreement about the score. Some said another man arrived, not involved in the game, to argue with a soldier about a girl he said was his. Others said that the wind switched directions, and as the afternoon grew late there was some bad air carried on the calls of the night birds who were just starting to wake up. However it started, it ended like this. There were shouts and then three Yuvut men jumped a soldier. A young one who sweated a lot. He was quickly dead, from one of the machetes, and then the rest of the soldiers started firing. The people of Yuvut ran; they hid in their huts and in the forest. They were fast and none of them were killed on that day, only some wounded shoulders and legs. But these would fester, infect and kill them more slowly later. Some may have thought the incident was over then. But it was not.

The government sent in more soldiers. And they didn't just send them to Yuvut, but all around the central valleys and into the lower highlands. They sent helicopters with machine-guns. They sent men who were willing to lock people in huts and burn them. This is what happened to Aben's father and older brothers. His mother took him into the forest and they waited until the smell of burning hair was gone before returning. Those were the times of the big killings.

---

Before Julia, after Julia. So far, all I had to measure by. So I chased the stories of the fighting, of the riots and the shootings. Tried to make them mine so that one day I might say that I was alive for those times, so I could have a rod to measure my life by. I felt like I was stealing the stories, using them to say something about myself — to be something bigger than I ever could be. Stuffing them inside my head like a rooster trying to fit too many corn kernels in his beak at once. Overflow and choke.

## TWENTY-ONE

The people in the medical handbook for foreigners living in third-world countries said that biting midge and mosquito activity peaks when the full moon rises and that we should stay away from pools of still water. They said that we should wear long pants and long sleeves whenever possible, and paint all exposed skin with the bug spray that stings if it gets on a cut or on sunburn or on a mosquito bite that is already there. But it was too hot for the long sleeves, and even if we wore them the bugs knew how to get through cloth and chemicals and screens. My father called them tiny Houdinis — minute magicians who always knew where to find us.

When the drought first started to fully reach Yuvut and make the clay near the edges of the creek crack and curl and its pools turn stagnant and smell, I woke in the dark and my body crawled with an ache so deep I felt it drilling, burrowing into bone.

In my stomach was an ice-cold knot or maybe a brick, because in seconds I felt it growing and I was desperate with that cold, cold and desperate, and I moaned for a fire to throw myself into. The burn would be worth it as long as it melted the ice. I thought that Julia had my hand and was leading me to this fire that might save me, but she stopped me from going in at the last moment. I hated her then and was jealous of the flames that bloomed at her feet like flowers that were too bright.

I fell back down into the darkness of sleep. I dreamed of spiders. I dreamed that they crawled up into the bed, over and up my feet: thorn-lined legs, a sea of eyes. They bit down on me as one. I half woke then and my legs burned with cramps. There was a swollen pinch in my groin and, almost pleasurable, the breaking warmth as my bladder emptied into the sheets, ran in hot streams down my legs. There was an itch as it cooled. Sleep's soft ropes pulled me back. There was another dream that told me I got up and changed the sheets, stood in the shower as heat rained down, cleaned up so it never happened. I was spotless. Sun-on-snow white, and faultless. But then the ache and cold woke me again to dampness.

Dengue fever was the disease, and its other name is Break Bone. Except the sharpness of an actual break would almost be a relief compared with the grinding pain that makes 'dull' a lie. It has been said that the blunt force of a crocodile's tooth can do more damage than a well-sharpened blade.

I vomited. But still I was flat on my back and my limbs were pinned by the fever to the bed and the vomit was thick in my hair, in my mouth, choking back down my throat, and yet my teeth were still rattling on account of the cold in my body. There was a smell of rotting strawberries and bitter bile. I could not see.

I was tired, oh so tired. The vomit was drying, caking on my face, stiffening against my lips. After everything, I heard myself thinking before all was dark again, it might just be easier to sleep.

---

In the morning I was lying on the hard sofa in the living room, the one that smelled of dust and age. My mother seemed nervous and continuously walked between the kitchen and me, only stopping to pour small cups of hoarded soft drink she asked Sonya to get from the pasar to settle my stomach. It will be better than water for you right now, Mum told me. It's for the electrolytes.

I think she said these things more for her sake than mine. Sometimes she rested her hand on the two-way radio and glanced at my father.

Soon the hospital will be built, he said, more times than he needed to, more times than he had before. Then problems like this will be a thing of the past.

He was having more trouble with the wood. They weren't bringing him enough and many of the planks were too small to be of any use. And there was bad news about the road, too. There was a landslide that killed two of the workers. It would take weeks to move the dirt and find the bodies to bury.

But it isn't the past now, said my mother. What the hell do I do now?

He did not have an answer for her, no matter how loud she got, no matter how many times she threatened to get up and leave, to push that button on the two-way radio and send her voice out searching for sense among the flight numbers and never-private conversations of that static world.

Just tell her something! I wanted to yell, and, in my haze, I thought I did. That is all my mother wanted. She didn't even need the perfect words; she just wanted someone else to have an answer, hold her hand.

On the fifth day a rash broke over my stomach and the name of the disease was confirmed (by my mother reading in her medical book). Dengue likes to mimic and accompany malaria, but malaria has no rash. Mum seemed calmer once the disease was named and cornered. She continued feeding me soft drinks, boiled potatoes with a little margarine, sometimes one of our precious eggs. I slept a lot. I decided that my bones might ache forever. I made my peace with this. I slept some more.

After I was out of bed, light on tender feet, Susumina took me down to the river again. We looked towards where the elbow was meant to be. I thought about running there then, of going while my body felt like it was still suspended between earth and sky. I could fly there; walk on the water so it couldn't draw me down into the depths. The pills I took made my ears ring and I could almost hear the bees from the creek on the day Julia and I jumped from the rocks.

One day we'll go there, I said.

One day, said Susumina.

I started to reach my hand towards hers, thinking she was Julia. But then I remembered and I stopped. The bees seemed to buzz on.

## PURPLE SHALLOTS
*Wamena, 1993*

*Joseph, age seven, knows the objects dangling above his head by their dried stems at the pasar as bawang merah. His mother, Laura, knows them as purple shallots, or sometimes — when she remembers her Hindi from when she was a child of missionaries as Joseph is now — as kaanda. Merah means red, and Joseph's mother wonders when and how one language decided that this sweet-sour part of the onion family was red while the other decided it was purple.*

*The owner of the bawang merah cuts them down and exchanges them with Laura for a ball of dirtied notes. Laura is always afraid to think of where those notes have been. Wamena, perched in the cool highlands of Irian Jaya, is a city (the largest entirely serviced by air, in fact), but it is a city that looks as if it was simply lowered down from the sky on top of and between villages that had been there for centuries. Which means that sometimes Laura and Joseph see men walking down the street beside the three-wheeled* becak *and motorcycles, dressed in nothing but a penis sheath. This horrified Laura at first until she realised that Joseph and his younger sister Rebecca did not share her horror because this is what they knew as normal and real in this place. Sometimes she tries to copy her children's calmness, but she just as often forgets.*

*Laura passes the shallots to Joseph to hold, and he takes her hand with his free one as they continue on through the* pasar *to find elusive carrots or even, if they are very lucky, a lettuce that Laura will soak in bleach to kill whatever germs she imagines might populate its leaves. Her own mother did this in India as well. Laura has forgotten what it is like to eat raw vegetables without the faint taste of bleach in her mouth. She wonders if Joseph will ever know any different either, perhaps taste the salads her brothers wax lyrical about now that they have settled back in their passport country in homes close to giant supermarkets bathed in fluorescent lights.*

*Joseph holds her hand tightly as they walk. He watches the people around them carefully. Many men, few women. His mother seems to be the only foreign woman here today. He knows his mother does not like the pasar. There have been fights and even murders in some sections. One week a man lunged forward and grabbed at Laura's chest before Joseph could place his body in between the man and his mother. Now he keeps even closer. His dad told him that he is big and strong and a good helper. Wamena, with its mountains and deep gutters on the sides of the roads, is what Joseph knows. It is all he knows, except for his parents' stories of other countries and one space of six months when they returned to another country people said was his home for Rebecca to be born. That was three years ago now, and Joseph remembers only the bear his grandparents got for him and how it used to make a sound when you squeezed its stomach hard.*

*They used to bring Rebecca with them to the pasar. When she was a baby and then a toddler she was strapped to Laura's chest and Laura felt invisible and safe behind that warm small body. But now she is older and will squirm and maybe even run in the pasar, and so Laura takes just Joseph instead, to hold her hand and her shallots. She has thought about another child, but both her husband and her church say that more children mean more money and other people get to have a say in the size of your family when they are paying the money for it in a velvet offering bag.*

*There are people in the pasar that Laura and Joseph know. At their stalls, Joseph lets go of Laura's hand and she talks to these people as they wrap up her purchases. But it is in the close corridor between stalls, down the middle of the pasar, and the dark warrens of stalls that go deeper off to the sides, that Laura feels like she stops being human and can no longer see others as human either. This is where Joseph feels her fear and where they hurry until they can leave the pasar, in the more open air, where people start to have faces again and Laura remembers that not everyone is a man who might tip forward towards her. She remembers how a man — back in her passport country — attacked her sister-in-law in a parking lot behind her office. How it can happen anywhere. She remembers that it is not just her in this place. There are other women, the same hurts as well as other hurts. But sometimes it is hard to remember these things. As they leave the pasar, she lets Joseph run ahead to blow on dandelions growing by the side of the road.*

*At home, Laura unpacks the vegetables she bought at the pasar and hands Joseph half of the bawang merah to take to Ibu Kristina, who lives in a triplex-boarded room across the fence from their back yard. They met Ibu Kristina on the day they first arrived in Wamena, when Joseph was just over a year old. Joseph was tired, and screamed and screamed in the house that Laura and her husband had just got the keys for, and as they stood helpless among boxes and wondered how to get the stove working, how to get the ant nests out from under the carpet, and where everything was. There was a knock at the door in the middle of one of Joseph's loudest screams. When it opened, Ibu Kristina smiled at Laura, who was holding Joseph, and gestured that she wanted to hold him. Laura was too tired to say no and too tired to even consider if this was normal. Ibu Kristina took Joseph out to the yard, where there were grasshoppers leaping through the unmown grass and a guava tree with just-ripening fruit. She played with him there until Laura and her husband had figured out where the sheets for the beds were, the plates and cups, and the sound of a kettle boiling signalled that all would be well because now they could cook a meal in their strange kitchen.*

*Since then, Ibu Kristina is often over, or Joseph is over at her place. She is a widow and lives on the little money that her eldest son sends from Sentani. She likes to watch reality TV and has a row of photos taped by her bed: all her children and grandchildren, the living and the dead. She teaches Laura how to use the ancient washing machine left behind by another missionary, and how to boil rice so it does not dry out and burn. Joseph likes to visit her especially when she is cooking her evening meal, because she teaches him how to use the different kinds of chillies, herbs, mysterious leaves that grow in her yard in patches. How to tell different kinds of bananas apart, how to make a fire with no matches. Joseph also watches Tom & Jerry cartoons on her TV.*

*She often cooks with bawang merah. She slices it up fine and deep-fries it as a garnish, or mixes it with shrimp paste and chillies and the dark kang-kung leaves in her hot wok. She knows how to pickle them, too, and this is the way Joseph likes them best. When Joseph breathes in this spicy-sharp smell he feels the same way he does when leaning against Ibu Kristina's stomach as they shell peanuts or sort laundry together. Like he knows where he belongs. Like she does not need him to hold her hand in the pasar but she might ask him to anyway.*

## TWENTY-TWO

My dad could slide the skins of rabbits right off. When he slid their skins off, their bodies were still hot and still bleeding. They looked like red jelly babies, babies who were born too dark and too young. Before he skinned them he cut a line around their ankles so they wouldn't catch when he took the rest of the skin off.

The rabbit-breeding programme was, according to Dad, a success. The rabbits we brought with us from the city multiplied and multiplied again. Twenty families got their own rabbits and those ones were multiplying, too. In our hutches lived the ten original rabbits: the core breeding group, as my parents called them. And we kept a few of the children rabbits for ourselves, killing one to eat every couple of weeks because the Australian mince had not lasted and no one came to our door selling other meat wrapped in banana leaves and smelling warm.

Every morning I gathered the dark sweet potato leaves and vegetable scraps to feed to the rabbits. They drank water out of empty butter tins and slept most of the time. Sometimes large bees, much bigger than the house ones which had become ordinary by now, swarmed near their cages. These bees had grey-blue bodies, and when they were near the rabbits Sonya didn't let me feed them. Those kinds of bees were too large and could sting a pig to death. But the rabbits didn't seem to mind them, and just waited by their cage doors for the next day when the bees would move on and they could have their vegetable scraps.

It was my job to keep an eye on the pregnant mother rabbits, too, to tell my parents when one of them went into labour. There was always at least one pregnant rabbit. They started the birthing part by moving around their nests, which were wooden boxes filled with grass clippings that I left in the corners of the cages. They licked themselves a lot and their eyes got larger right before the babies were born. Then some of the mothers did what they were supposed to do. But some of them did not. Sometimes they were afraid and ate their babies or kicked them out of the nest and left them to shiver to death on the bare chicken wire. Sometimes big red and black ants came and chewed away the babies' eyes before we could flick them away.

The first time a mother rabbit abandoned her babies, Susumina and I tried to save them. We took the tiny brown-pink bodies and put them on our bare chests under our shirts. Nails, still soft, grazed against my skin, and there was a tremor that could be a breath. But the babies, seven of them this time, shivered to death as if we were not helping them at all. One by one they died with our fingers cupping them. Susumina shrugged. That's what happens, she said.

It's stupid, I said. I did not want to feel guilty for any more deaths. I named them by the days of the week because they were seven. We buried them in a row of graves near the pit where Sonya burned our rubbish once a week, and decorated the graves with lollipop wrappers and the dried petals I saved from a rose my father tried to grow for my mother to remind her of New Zealand, though the plant eventually died from something eating up its stems at night. Susumina and I stood in front of the graves and together we sang a half-chant, half-wail to send off the baby rabbit spirits properly.

What now? said Susumina afterwards. We hunted for eggs for my mother because the chickens were sneaky and found new places every week. Then we got distracted by the ant-lion pits in the silt under the house, and crouched in the dirt catching ants and feeding them to the ant lions that we never saw.

There could be rats under there, my father said when he saw us. Or snakes, or spiders. We ignored him.

It's funny, I told Susumina. When we're under the house, my parents are the ones warning us of snakes and things, and when we're up a tree it's the Yuvut people who yell and tell us to get down before we are bitten by something. Adults in Yuvut did not seem to trust the trees.

No one knows what they're talking about, said Susumina. She caught an extra-large bull ant and sent it to its fate.

---

Then there was the day the rabbit cried and the man laughed. On this day, my dad was at the hospital site again, and Dani who cut our grass with his machete sometimes, and who helped my father with the water tanks, had the job of killing the rabbit for dinner for my mother. Susumina and I always watched the killing. We did not know why, but we had not learnt to be afraid of it yet. It still seemed like a game to us.

Dani took one of the boy rabbits, the one with a black spot on his side, to the laundry shed, and we followed. The killing was always meant to be the same: one twist of the neck and the rabbit was limp and it was over and my father could get to the skinning.

But this time Dani twisted and there was a pause. And then somewhere there was the sound of a high thin cry. There was no other sound but this. A baby, perhaps? And then Susumina thought it was a goat's kid that was lost on the airstrip. And then our ears began to understand where the sound was coming from and it was the rabbit and it was still alive but could not move and it cried and cried. Susumina jumped back and yelled, and then there were tears in my eyes and I ran and hid in the house, behind my mother who did not know why I was crying. But in my ears the cry kept on going and never stopped.

Outside, I heard Dani put the rabbit, now dead, on the porch for my mother. He laughed and shook his head as he walked out the gate. And that was how I knew the doctors lied when they said that Julia did not suffer in the three days before she died. She might have cried and my ears were just not there to hear it.

My mother said that those rabbits were always tough. She boiled and boiled them but still the meat clung to the bones.

There was another reason, other than snakes, why the people in Yuvut did not like the trees, or some of the trees anyway. They did not like the ones the fireflies flew from, the ones that looked like they could be trees strung with Christmas lights at night.

We're here to cut the tree down by the front gate, two men, Susumina's relatives, told my father.

Why?

Because that's where some of the spirits of the dead are getting caught as they try to leave the burial hill. Haven't you seen their eyes that glow in the night?

The men looked at my father as if everyone knew that, as if they did not believe someone could be so stupid not to know that.

They're just insects, said Dad. He made a buzzing sound. Everyone looked at him like he was crazier than usual. Never mind, he said. But you can't chop the tree down. It's ours.

When I washed the dishes at night I watched the fireflies through the window. Little people eyes, old people eyes, maybe baby rabbit eyes. All who got snagged in the branches of the tree when they were just trying to find their way to Heaven or Hell. Eyes, eyes everywhere. In the trees, waiting. On the ground if they fell, watching until their lights went out. In Yuvut, if an elder sibling died, the spirit had a place to go — into the younger sibling. But if a younger sibling died, that spirit had nowhere to go except for maybe getting caught in the firefly tree or turning into an animal. Or even worse — lying alone with their eyes fading in the dirt.

*Dear Grandad,*

*Here is what I learned from the guidebook lately. Fireflies are not flies. They belong to the beetle family. They sometimes eat each other. You told me that girl praying mantises eat boy praying mantises after they mate so that the girl has enough energy to grow her eggs into babies. The girl fireflies do this to the boy fireflies, too. Even after mating, she keeps pretending that she is looking for a mate just so she can keep on eating.*

*There are lots of different kinds of fireflies. The boy fireflies like to display their lights together, and they usually stick to the same spots. They can create light without creating heat. This is called bioluminescence (I learned how to spell this, but I still had to look at the book to get it right when I was writing). Mum says fireflies are one of the few creatures that live on land that can do this. Most things that can create light in this way live in the ocean. Probably because it is darker under water than on land.*

*Do we have fireflies in New Zealand? I can't remember.*
*Love, Ruth*

## TWENTY-THREE

The old lady who brought us watermelons and sweet potatoes on her back died, and the tree grew thicker with fireflies. Her hut that she shared with her youngest son and his family was on the other side of the airstrip, near the church, and we could hear the sound of her relatives gathering there and crying together. An early evening fog settled on the grass and even this did not muffle the wails that sounded as though they were rising from the earth to float up through the white.

Blink, went the fireflies.

She didn't die of malaria or any other disease in the pamphlets that we kept trying to hand out. Just old age, I think, my father told my mother. Mum did not cry, just finished chopping the onions for a stew and tossed them in a cast-iron pot on top of the stove. I'm sorry, my father said. He stood behind her with his hands in his pockets, looking like he didn't know what to do, and this made me afraid like I was afraid when I saw him standing above Julia's bed in the hospital the last time I saw her.

Why are you sorry? She was old, like you said. My mother began on the carrots that were brought in on a plane the week before from a place in the mountains where it was cool enough for them to grow. Yet still they were stunted copies of how I remembered carrots should be.

I hovered in the kitchen doorway, scuffing my bare feet on the dusty boards because Sonya was over on the other side of the airstrip all day with the mourners and therefore no one had kept up with the sweeping. If the air was allowed to be still for just moments in Yuvut it seemed that the dust started falling, started collecting in the corners, on the soles of our feet.

You're both getting in the way, said my mother, pushing past to get into the freezer. Go keep yourselves occupied in the lounge.

My father and I obeyed.

She'll be okay, my father said. But we could not keep our eyes on our books, and instead we stared through the window mesh into the fog as it, and the voices in it, threatened to seep through the house. When I leaned my head against the wall, the boards seem to hum with those voices. I was not afraid any more, though. I wanted to be out there with them.

---

Funerals happened quickly in Yuvut because there was no refrigeration for the bodies in those sorts of places. And definitely no coroner like on TV, no polished coffins with red velvet insides. Three days after the old lady died, the pigs for the funeral meal arrived from the village she left when she got married years ago. The old lady would be wrapped in one of her blankets and carried out in the arms of her son to the stack of wood that her family had been collecting since she died. The wood would already be on fire before she was laid on it. This was her ending because she had lived a whole life, and the burial hill and graves were kept for those children and young wives whose relatives could not bear to see them burn. Julia was both burned and buried. I do not know what this says about the wholeness of her life.

Do we wear black or not? asked my mother. I've only got a black skirt and this camisole, and the skirt is too tight to sit on the ground. She waved lace at my father.

Everyone else just seems to wear the same clothes they wear every day, Dad said. He held up a tie in the mirror. He brought three to Indonesia, thinking they might be needed for church, for meetings. All three were creased from never having been unpacked until the old lady's funeral. One was the one he wore to Julia's burial, the burial I did not go to.

Honestly? said Mum. You know a tie will stick out like a sore thumb.

They left — my father tie-less and my mother with a black ribbon tied around her wrist, just in case.

I stayed behind and listened to the cries of the old woman's family. The pigs were killed as more relatives arrived. I imagine that people who buy their meat from supermarkets expect and hope that the moments between life and death are quick. And it is for some. But for others there are moments called dying, and those pigs knew those moments because an arrow in the heart allowed for bleed-out time, screaming time. From the window I heard some of the children, Susumina with them perhaps, talking as they waited for the pigs to finish.

Then the rocks were heated for the cooking pits. The people who picked the rocks were careful, but once upon a time this land used to be made by volcanoes, and sometimes a rock left over from that time got mixed in with the others and when it heated up it exploded in shards because of the air pockets trapped in it. When this happened, the young men who turned the rocks with long sticks split halfway to make giant tongs jumped back and laughed at their own surprise and fear.

I knew when the pits were filled and covered because I could smell the meat and the vegetables, imagine them softening. Across the airstrip, in the churchyard where the funeral and feast were being held, the bright skirts of women spread like flowers in the dirt as they sat to tend the pits and their babies. Polyester flashed in the sun. Most of the women would have half-finished string bags in their laps that they would knit in between wiping a child's face, kicking away a dog that got too close.

Before the cooking pits were broken open for everyone to eat, the funeral fire's flames reached so high into the sky they looked like they might consume the one tree that stood outside the church's entrance. Then the voices all of a sudden rose, scared the lorikeets in our yard to silence. The body must have been carried out. It must have been going, gone.

I still watched the flames. Then the voices slipped quieter, the smell of the cooking pits in the wind got stronger. I made myself a Milo and waited for my parents to come home.

My parents' clothes were stained with sweat and clay. Mum had lost the black ribbon somewhere. Her neck was sunburnt and already turning tan like the backs of her hands always were.

I'll make you a sandwich, Ruth, said my mother. We're full, but it's good you didn't come. It would have been a bit too much.

Susumina came to the door as I ate my sandwich. Look, she said. She had stolen the bladder from one of the pig carcasses, blown it into a white balloon for us to play with. We kicked it between ourselves in the yard until the fruit bats started flying out for the night.

## TWENTY-FOUR

On the day of Julia's funeral, Grandma Rose stayed back with me, making Louise cake and scones to pass the time. The house was cold and the wind came under the door in the kitchen. We pressed close to the stove for its heat. I remember a ginger cat outside, not ours, and how the raspberry jam bled into the cake. While our cake baked we stood at the sink licking batter off the spoons and watching the sun that made it look like a much warmer day than it was. Are you okay? I asked my grandmother. It seemed like the right thing to say on a funeral day. She brushed my hair back instead of answering.

Grandma Rose's old Bible lived under a dusty doily on her bedside table. As a child she had been able to decipher the Afrikaans words inside, translate the sounds that looked to me like an alien was seeking to communicate to anyone who might be out there spinning alone in space. I used to believe that if one word, just one word, could lodge in someone's ear and stick, maybe this would change everything. Or maybe it would change nothing. By the time Rose left school, though, the mother tongue was lost, washed away by a monolingual school and parents who subsided quickly into English.

In the space left behind by those words, she grew stories for Julia and me, and collected her stones, amulets, little objects bought from roadside stalls, picked up in junk shops. Things she believed were so pretty or strange that they must have a meaning hidden deep under their lacquer, varnish, plastic beads.

My grandmother didn't discriminate between kinds of stories, though. The Grimm brothers, Hans Christian Andersen, the Bible, old murder ballads half-remembered from her own grandmother who was Scottish (unmoored in Africa and married to a man who didn't speak the same language as her, with children who spoke different languages again). All were fair game for my grandmother and for us, all those stories that seemed so disconnected from anything solid in our lives but that we tried to grab onto.

Julia liked the Brothers Grimm the best. Her favourite was the story of Jorinda and Joringel, because of the nightingales and the purple flower. She liked princesses who won their princes and witches who died skewered in nail-studded barrels. She liked justice. But those brothers seemed to tell too many stories about sisters, always one good and one bad. Always the good one won and the bad one lost, and when Julia cheered because the elder sister's head got chopped off, I sat and leaned against my grandmother's cushions, rubbing bald spots in their velvet and wondering how the bad sister got that way and if anyone cared.

My favourites were the Bible stories, version NLV from the English family Bible my grandparents kept in their living room.

But I only liked the way my grandmother told its stories. When Rose told those stories they were no longer black and white print on sheets of paper so thin you could almost see through them. She gave them the colour that the printed pages always seem to steal. She gave them music and silks, beaded hair, hearts that beat, warm blood. And so I chased after Eve, Hagar, Rahab and, of course, Ruth. I collected them like witnesses, as if one day I might need to pile them in a stack before God and Julia. Look, see? I might say. Convict them if you must convict me. Even if I did not know what I might ever get convicted of.

My mother, Miriam, and her mother, Rose, had a relationship, their own kind of being together. Through Rose, Miriam learned about guardian angels and amber, lapis lazuli and others. Ways of calling for help and ways of praying for things you should not. But Rose also knew how to keep grudges down in her gut, and how to perfectly place her second-language words so that they might do the most hurt. Theirs was not a relationship broken by one event, one definite mark on a timeline. It was one that collapsed slowly like a circus tent, gently caving in the middle. It was Miriam sending ginger slice, her mother's favourite, with me when I visited. It was Rose asking me if Miriam was still watching *Shortland Street* on TV. It was both women looking out of windows while I ran between two houses.

The night Julia was born, I was lifted from my bed and carried to my grandparents' house while I pretended to sleep, keeping myself limp so that I could lean my head against my grandfather's chest for longer. This is either my own memory or something I have been told. Grandad tucked me into the spare-room bed. He felt more crumpled than he did in daylight; his chin was unfamiliar and prickled when he kissed my forehead.

The next day I was carried back to the yellow house (the birth of siblings was a good excuse to be held, I found), and Julia lay curled, wrinkled, red, in a bassinet by my parents' bed, next to Mum propped up with pillows. Julia was born feet first, making the labour longer and harder, leaving my mother emptier in more ways than one afterwards.

Sometimes in the mornings in Yuvut I went to see my mother like I did in the yellow house. At that time of day, she seemed leached of colour. I had the urge to fill her up with something to make her look less *less* and worn. I started bringing tea to her. Sometimes I spilled a little tea on her nightgown when I handed it to her, not enough to burn but enough to stain, to see if she might react or not. Most times she did not.

No old lady meant no sweet potatoes and onions for my mother. No watermelons, corn, lessons on how to keep ants from coming up between the floorboards. No one to hold her hands, both of them at the same time. After the funeral, my mother didn't even like to go as far as the porch, and there were no outside walks on Sundays. She read the two *House & Garden* magazines that she brought from New Zealand so often that the pages became thin with creases. The tea bags were running low, so she used one a day and made it last for five cups or more. She even stopped asking Dad about the hospital. She did not ask him anything when he came in at the end of the day, just waited until he had finished with the bucket shower, then handed him a glass of water.

For a few days I tried to stay in as well. I finished my schoolwork more slowly, asked her questions that I knew the answers to. You'll figure it out, Ruth, she said. I know you will. I'll be in the lounge if you need me.

After a week, with her still curled in the lounge drinking pale tea and trying to hold all her pages together, I didn't try any more. I ran out of the gate and down to the airstrip where Susumina and the others had the football.

## TWENTY-FIVE

A fresh batch of policemen arrived. I could hear them get off the plane with their boxes of noodles and bags of rice as I sat at my desk, writing a journal entry for the teacher in New Zealand who, every few months, sent me back my work covered with stickers that shouted WOW! in rainbows, and wrote comments like 'That sounds very interesting' and 'You have a great imagination!' The policemen's rifles shone so bright in the sun that I could see them from the window. They looked fake, like plastic water-guns for children who liked to pretend they were the real thing.

Who's this? the new policemen asked when I went down to the airstrip to play football that afternoon. So pale, so pretty! What's your name, little girl?

No one, I said, and grabbed the ball off Susumina, ready to run with it into the grass.

Wait, said one policeman. He looked the youngest of all of them, with short black hairs trying to be a moustache on his top lip. You want a lollipop? I'll give you a lollipop.

No, I said, and I tried to leave again. I didn't feel like playing the game I was supposed to play today, the game where I smiled and let my cheeks get pinched.

The policeman grabbed Susumina's arm.

Come on, he said. I bet your friend wants a lollipop. Don't you? He pulled her into his lap and, too quick, his hands were under her skirt where I knew no underpants were. Susumina started to pull away, but another policeman put his hand on her shoulder, fingers firm enough to leave marks that showed up later, but he still smiled.

*Jangan*! I said. Don't! You're all just old men.

Old men who smell bad, said Susumina. The hands were still under her skirt and she said the words like she was having fun, but there was sweat on her forehead and she still pulled against the hands.

Let us give you a lollipop, said the young policeman. Then you girls can go play your game.

Okay, I said. Just one lollipop for me and one for Susumina.

I stepped forward. The policeman reached in his money pouch for the lollipops. Susumina got off his lap and stood by me. As he handed me one, he reached with his other hand and pinched my cheek hard. Just a lollipop! I said, as I slapped his hand. The other policemen laughed. But the young one did not.

What are you doing to my daughter? I heard these words in English. The words didn't seem to fit here. They moved in the wrong way through the air. My mother walked towards us down the path from our house. She wore the leather sandals that she used to wear in New Zealand. Now they looked too new.

Some of the policemen had not seen her before because she left the house so rarely. Some stood up to get a better look.

It's okay, Mum. They think I'm lucky.

The other children on the airstrip watched now. Women walking home from their sweet potato gardens giggled behind their hands as they passed.

Lucky! My mother shook her hands in the young policeman's face. You don't touch a child in that way.

The policeman didn't smile again. He grabbed my mother's hand, twisted her wrist and crushed her fingers in his so hard that she dropped to her knees.

Go home, foreigner, he said in his language, then let her go.

Mum got up and held her hand against her chest. I was not sure if she knew the word for foreigner yet. Come on, Ruth, she said. There were tears on her cheeks that I knew she didn't mean to be there. I wondered if maybe she had been watching me all along, all those months, from the window, just like I watched the policemen arrive on the plane. I thought of the bees that bumped against the screen windows, trying to get out.

It's okay, Mum. I'll come home soon.

I thought she was going to ask me again, and maybe if she had then I would have said yes and followed her, but she didn't, just walked back up the path and through the gate.

The policemen ignored Susumina and me now, and started tossing stones at an empty Coke can, seeing who could hit it first. I gave my lollipop to one of the other girls who came to play football.

When I returned to the house at dinner time, the stove was cold, the wood unlit, and my mother was in her bedroom with the door closed.

My father yelled. No more football, no more policemen. Then he went back to his radios. Mum didn't say much. Afterwards I used the peanut-butter jar for my shouts. But, still, anger sat in the back of my throat, large and sticky.

I went out to the back shed where the pile of wood for the stove sat next to the new generator that my father paid too much for to make my mother smile and believe that we could survive anywhere. There were two axes. One tall, one short. One for the big pieces of wood, one for the kindling that burned quick and pale. I held the short axe. Dad had said the week before that it was blunt, that he needed to sharpen it, that he would get around to it one day. I liked how it felt in my hands. The wood handle varnished and smooth, the weight of the steel head that tipped it forwards. It felt real. Solid. Forever.

I got a twig and chopped it. I made a miniature bonfire out of the splinters. Then I looked at my finger resting on the stump that was the kindling's chopping block and for a moment the finger wasn't mine. It was my father's, and the rage carried through me, down my arm, into the axe.

There was a brief space of time when the cut was only surprised flesh, a peek of bone, enough time to think, Oh, our bones really are white, too — and then the cleft filled with red. Clotted bubble. It became mine again. Tears began, but there was no one to hear me so they seemed wasted somehow. It was only a small cut, in the end. The axe was too blunt to do more, and the bone was close to the skin.

I examined the cut edges of my skin. Half of Susumina's grandmother's fingers were all stubs. Once upon a time little girls and sometimes little boys in Yuvut sacrificed a joint of one of their fingers for each close relative who died. They sometimes even cut their own ears or their own hair and tossed these pieces of their bodies up on the thatch of their roofs. At this time, though, if it happened at all, it was just teenage girls who did it for their mothers, boyfriends, husbands. But you still saw old ladies, the occasional old man, with their fingers all stubs, which told others without words of all their losses, of how bad the grief hurt, and of how their older relatives cut them to try to keep death from following any more relatives home. The finger cutting could be done by biting, by tourniquet, by axe or machete. And even the women who had nothing but their thumbs left could still somehow make their string bags while sitting by the cooking pits or by the airstrip, waiting for the planes to come in.

I thought about trying again with the axe, trying to punish my father more that way. But instead I left the axe in the shed, went back into the house and walked past my father in the kitchen with the edge of my tee-shirt twisted around the finger to soak up the blood. I wrapped it in gauze and plasters in the bathroom.

What did you do to yourself? asked my mother when I came out. She was still trying.

Just scraped myself on a nail.

Good thing you've had your tetanus shot, I guess.

A few weeks earlier, four men carried a stretcher out of the bush to our house with another man lying on it. They had made the stretcher out of a blanket and wooden poles, like the ones they used to hang the pigs on, alive or dead. The man on the stretcher had cut himself with a rusty razor. Now he couldn't open his mouth, and his arms and legs were clenched up and could not move. Mum, reading from her medical book, said he had tetanus. He went away on a plane that came to take him to a hospital in the city. Dad said he died there. The man had a striped beanie that was all sorts of colours. I wondered if it was just going to be thrown away at that hospital or if someone else got to keep it.

Put some antibiotic cream on your finger before you go to bed, said my mother. Then, to my father, for the first time in weeks, How is the hospital coming? There was grit in her voice, like shale starting its slide down a mountain's face.

There's a thing about secrets: they always make one person powerful and one person weak. This one, for a short time, made me powerful.

## LICHEN
*Twenty kilometres outside of Sarmi, 2003*

*I found part of this story in a newspaper article. The rest comes from rumour.*

*Under a bridge on the road between Sarmi and Sentani there is a car. It is the kind they call Kijang in Indonesia: a strong Toyota bred especially for Indonesia's kinds of landscapes. Reliable, good for getting through potholes, rivers, the occasional small landslide. This Kijang, though, is not moving. It rests with its nose down in the riverbed (which dried up long ago), but other than some dents in the front it doesn't seem too badly damaged. All four doors hang wide open.*

*The underside of the bridge is all crusted with lichen and velveted with moss. It arches over the Kijang, and the light through the trees casts everything green and gold. Chunks of concrete lie in the riverbed, fallen from the bridge at some point. Against one, the bodies of a man and his wife lean. The official report will say that there was a car accident. They simply did not cross the bridge as slowly as they should have. They went right through the railing. That is what the report will say once it is filed at the Sentani police station, written into a newspaper story and then forgotten.*

*The family were travelling between Sarmi and Sentani after selling a piece of land in Sarmi. It was a large piece of land, and the payment was in cash. Banks are still rare creatures in the more remote areas of Papua. So the family had the cash in their Kijang and they were on their way back from Sarmi to Sentani to deposit their earnings and carry on with their lives. Their relatives in Sarmi didn't know they were missing for two weeks because they said goodbye and thought the family must have made it to Sentani safe and sound. Their relatives in Sentani didn't know they were missing for two weeks because they thought the family were in Sarmi selling their land, and who knew how long that could take.*

*So it is not until someone else from Sarmi has to make the trip between there and Sentani on the damp and slippery, mostly empty road that anyone notices the Kijang in the riverbed and can carry the news with them to Sentani.*

*When the family come to collect the bodies, they see the man and woman. Their throats each have one cut. Their deaths look as if they were swift. But it is the children they do not see at first. Two children, a boy and a girl. Ten and eleven years old. The family do not see them until someone points up. And there are the children, hanging, swinging from a tree by the bridge. Their bodies are light as paper. And all over, everywhere, there are ants and the lichen creeping.*

## TWENTY-SIX

I woke up to the sound of my mother throwing plates against the wall.

You said we would be gone by now! I heard through the wall. You said we could go home!

The day was one circled on a calendar, with an army of felt-tip Xs leading up to it: a year and three months since Julia died in the hospital under gauze and blank sheets. The circle marked a day when my father hoped the Yuvut hospital would be built enough to pass it on to someone else. It marked a day when my mother thought we might be lining up with our bags on the airstrip, weighing our suitcases along with chickens and peanuts being sent to the city. She thought we could leave Yuvut on this day, leave and never come back, and that soon after she might stretch out her arms in cooler air and let the curtains of the yellow house back in Nelson fly wide open. I wondered if it was a day she might use to leave Dad and me behind in that same yellow house, while she took herself and her coral nail polish and pearl earrings far, far away. She must have known, deep down, that we were not leaving Yuvut on this day. As long as there were unmarked days before the circle, though, there was hope and she had kept her anger covered.

But now the circled day arrived and there we were, still in this village as drought settled deeper into every crevice. The dust was rising thick and the creek had slowed and would slow further soon. The toilet stopped flushing and my father went to the swamp each morning to bring back buckets of water getting thicker with leaves and mosquito larvae. Fish got stranded as the water level dropped. The birds were happy and full, for now. Eels, shorter and fatter than the ones I used to know, skins painted slick with the mud that bubbled up with them from between the tree roots, were revealed.

For a year my parents had kept their rage washed over with energy to pass out pamphlets, to breed rabbits, to grow avocado trees and a hospital. They had pressed down their anger long enough even to hold hands on Sundays, to reach out to touch each other's backs, to pretend that we were a close three-person family.

As I lay in bed I heard the screen door swing shut, my father's footsteps leave the porch. The shower of ceramic and glass continued.

But noise followed my father to the hospital site. Dad found tools missing from the shed that he locked every night. He did not have the only key. From the lounge my mother and I heard people yelling back and forth from the direction of the site.

Angry or not, this time? my mother asked. The broken plates were swept onto the porch. Mum put everything not broken back on the shelves and tied her hair in a too-tight ponytail. Then she folded laundry and I stuck close, watching for whatever happened next.

This time the yelling is angry, I said. Because there aren't enough gaps between the yelling.

My mother kept folding laundry while I looked out the window and waited to see my father walk up the path and come home.

When he came through the door he seemed large and heavy, hot with anger. Dirt was smeared down his arms, and the knuckles on his right hand were grazed from where they rubbed against the planks of wood all day. His left hand was wrapped in his handkerchief, blood seeping through, smears of blood on his legs below the hem of his shorts. I held my own hand against my chest, wondering if my anger and the axe earlier had translated into pain for my father. This gave me a brief thrill, tainted with fear at my own power.

What happened? said my mother, and she moved towards him.

He didn't talk to us, but went to the bathroom and started pouring water over his hand from one of the swamp buckets. We watched from the door, and when he took the handkerchief away we saw that the tip of one of his finger pads was missing. He had that tip still in the handkerchief as it came away. Blood dripped into the sink. My mother went into the bathroom and took the handkerchief with the bit of finger from my father. I could see the rage leaving him almost as fast as the blood. He no longer seemed as large. I held my finger again, wrapped in gauze, feeling guilt somewhere deep, in the same place I felt it when Julia burned and I remembered that doll.

I'll put this in the fridge, said my mother. Maybe it can be sewn back on.

She left the fingertip on the handkerchief and placed it in one of the carefully hoarded, washed and re-washed Ziploc bags that we brought with us from New Zealand. Two weeks later, while we were dumping everything that could rot from the house, and stuffing our lives back in suitcases, we found that bag in the back of the fridge with the tip of the finger turned grey and hard. I could still see the ridges that used to make up part of my father's fingerprint.

What do you need? she asked Dad now. What do you want?

Someone stole the skill-saw and a drill from the shed, he said. No one was saying anything but someone had to have done it. No one was listening and I didn't know what to do. I got out the electric planer so I could at least get some work done today, started up the generator and planed wood until I accidentally planed the top of my finger. The blood got them to pay attention, anyway.

My mother reached for his right hand and both my parents sat on the linoleum bathroom floor that was all bubbled at its edges. She pulled a towel from its rung and wrapped it around the wounded finger. My father already had a strip of fabric from his shirt tied around the base of it to stop the blood.

We have bandages, Mum said. When the blood stops we'll bandage it. It'll heal.

Then they were quiet except for the rattle of my father's keys hanging from his belt, which was the only clue that he shook.

I felt out of place in the hallway, watching them sit together, facing the world against everyone else. I left. My parents didn't say anything.

Susumina met me at the gate. Did you see? she said.

❦

As I left our yard it was like the aches of my illness were back, the ache of a broken bone under a cast that you wanted to rub at but couldn't, and we went to the burial hill to get away from it all. No football there, no policemen, no parents. So there should be no guilt.

Yacob joined us as we neared the top. We settled into the red dust and crossed our legs and looked out over the airstrip, listening for the drones of engines in the sky and predicting before they passed whether they might land or not. None of them landed this time.

Susumina made twists in my hair, like how some of the older girls wore it, and tied them with different colours of string. A breeze stirred the dust under our feet, but if we faced the right way it didn't get in our eyes. We sent our prayers to the few wisps of clouds in the distance that they might join together and bring rain.

Susumina had snuck some little pink jellies in their sealed plastic cones from someone (she wouldn't say who) and she passed them out. They were really only big enough for a mouthful, but we sucked on them slowly and let the flies rest on our toes and rub their tongues with their thin black wires for legs.

Yacob had his hand by the waistband of his shorts and he scuffed his feet in the dirt and made the dust worse. Stop it! said Susumina, and slapped his shoulder. Yacob grinned. He brought out his hand, and in it was a packet of cigarettes, the kind the policemen smoked and the kind that was not sold at the market.

Susumina and I drew the air between our teeth the way we saw the old women do at the market when they were not pleased.

Where did you get those? Susumina asked.

Just around, said Yacob. He took a cigarette out of the packet and brought it to his lips, pretending to suck on it.

Don't be stupid, said Susumina. But Yacob lit the cigarette anyway and tried to puff it like the policemen did, leaning back with one hip cocked. He coughed and blew the smoke our way.

Idiot, I said.

Try it, said Yacob.

You just want us to cough, too.

Try it, he said.

Susumina nodded and reached out her hand. She passed it to me and I rested it on my bottom lip. But there was too much sweat smell mixed in with cigarette smell and I could not get the policemen and their damp hands, damp uniforms, out of my head.

Here, take it, I told Susumina. She did and crushed it with her foot.

All idiots, she said. I prefer ones I can make myself. Anyway, if we are going to be football players they are no good at all.

Yacob laughed and put the rest of the packet away. We watched the wisps trying to be clouds again and we forgot all about cigarettes and blood and policemen.

Then later, after we left the hill, we turned and saw it on fire.

It was about four in the afternoon when the burial hill caught on fire. When my mother looked out of the kitchen window, between the curtains she had been trying to hide behind, the flames had already covered the entire side that faced away from the airstrip. When the men washing down in the creek finally heard the crackling above the sound of their splashes, the whole thing was covered. The drought had bleached the grass blond and dry. The red clay pressed over the graves on the hill had been cracked for weeks, maybe months. The men ran to nearby houses in their towels. There was a lot of running, a lot of buckets, but in the end they all just stood with their buckets and watched the flames, because there was nothing anyone could do about the hill and the graves on the hill. The fire would burn itself out on the rocks before it reached any homes, so now all they — all we — could do was watch.

It was after six and dark, except for embers that blinked like eyes on the hillside, when someone found the child with burns down her legs and lower back. They carried the child to her mother. It was then that the cries of her relatives began and everything was all chaos and noise like when lava tips over a cliff into the sea and turns to rock and steam.

My mother sat Marilina, the girl with the burnt legs, on our porch and painted her with something brown to kill bacteria. Strips of dead skin hung down like papery bark on a tree and my mother used her embroidery scissors to trim them back. This whole time Marilina never cried but only looked down at the floor. I didn't remember Julia crying either.

I handed my mother bandages so she could wrap Marilina's legs with them. My mother's fingers tried their best to barely graze her. At the back of my mind tugged the pale memory of my father putting Julia and me to bed, whipping the sheets high and letting them float back down to kiss our legs softly. When Julia was in the hospital, I wanted to do this for her. Do it with a sheet made of spider webs so soft and fine that its touch wouldn't hurt the raging burned skin.

Marilina's father came to carry her home when we were done. Will she be okay? I asked my mother. She didn't answer me. I wondered if she knew about the cigarettes. I wondered if she knew about the finger, too. And I wondered if she, all along, had known about the doll, and how I couldn't save Julia at the river or from the fire, and if she knew that I would never be enough for her now.

Later, in bed, I heard the water running in the bathroom. For a week we had only been allowed half a bucket of water a night to wash with. This time the water ran and ran, and through the sound of the water I heard my mother's sobs, seeping through our house like bats flooding out of a cave. I found Elizabeth the cat next to the bed. I clutched her to me and the claws on her good feet scratched and dug into my arms and chest while her damaged foot just hung there uselessly. She struggled and struggled until I had blood on my arms. Her muscles stretched and pulled under her fur. But I did not let go. I sang the lullaby my mother once sang to me, remembering more of its lines without even meaning to — *Sometimes you are sad, and sometimes I am sad, but I don't want that for you . . . Because I love you . . . you know I love you . . .*

Elizabeth yowled in the dark.

## TWENTY-SEVEN

The next day, Susumina and I went down to the river. We stopped by the spot where people fished. We dipped our toes in, and I sat back against a large rock and scribbled faces on it with a bit of charred wood from an old cooking fire.

But Susumina did not sit with me. She stood with her hands on her hips and looked downriver, down towards the first of the big bends even though we could not see that bend because it was about an hour's walk away. We remembered we were not supposed to talk about, think about, know about the bend, even though everyone told the stories. In Yuvut, the places we did not know about were unknown for reasons.

Someone else with other cigarettes might have been the cause of the fire, not us. Or cigarettes might not have started the fire at all. Just hot air and a spark, a wind that picked up at just the right time. We didn't know. Susumina had checked on Marilina that morning and told me that the little girl had not slept all night out of pain.

Someone else might have saved Julia. And who could have known that she would trip? That her nightgown would burn that quick and that my feet would be weighted to the earth and the screams wouldn't come from my mouth fast enough? I didn't know.

Let's go, I said. I had been watching the rapids, and for a minute, if I looked at them just right, they made me feel like I was being carried along with them. The river was lower than it used to be, but still it resisted El Niño and flowed deep in some places.

What?

Let's go. To the river's elbow!

Susumina laughed like people do when they don't believe something or are so shocked they don't know what else to do but laugh because the alternative is crying or horror.

We can't, she said. Not like she was angry or sad, but like it was a fact.

Why not?

Because! Because the old men say so. What's the point, anyway?

Well, I'm going. You don't have to come.

Until then I was only half-serious, half-joking. But after I said this I knew more than anything else that I had to get to the bend in the river. I got up from the bank and started walking.

I'll just follow the river, I said. I did not look behind me.

The further I walked along the edge of the river, the fewer feet seemed to have pressed down the grass and brush sprouting from the sides. The weeds whipped my shins red. This only made me walk faster. It was late afternoon and quiet because most fishermen had finished their work in the morning to avoid the heat, and there were fewer bathers these days. In pockets, where the trees blocked the wind, the air was so still and thick that I thought I might comb my fingers through it, part it like the Red Sea as my body moved through. I heard the swish of another body behind me in the grass. Susumina had followed. I still did not look behind.

We passed patches where pigs, wild ones, had been digging. Though there had been no rain, somehow water had collected in their footprints. I heard a bubbling somewhere in the undergrowth, hinting at a spring that resisted the drought. Worms rolled under broken roots. Mosquitoes hovered, the big kind with black-and-white-striped back legs. Susumina slapped one and the sound of her hand against her skin echoed through the trees. Somewhere, something bolted off into the leafy darkness. From the corners of my eyes, I caught glimpses of movement and colours as I walked. I assigned them to objects, animals. The jewelled red of a young tree python. Furred caterpillars that I was not supposed to touch. So many things lined with thorns and spines: plants, insects, reptiles. Everything trying to survive, stepping on the heads of everything else, all fighting for that one drop of water, sunshine, life.

We passed a small dam made for catching fish. Half of it had toppled into the shallows. It hadn't been used for a long time. But the river was getting deeper even without the dam. Somewhere along the walk it had turned another shade of green. Its surface was smooth, deceiving us into thinking it ran slow, but a leaf carried swiftly by told us of the current that moved underneath. I felt a leech settle behind my knee but did not stop to pick it off yet. Everything was damp, defying the drought that chewed at the forest edges. The high-pitched whine and rasp of a cicada cut through the heated afternoon hush.

We were close. I was close. Susumina was quiet now. And then — a break in the bush, a curve in the bank, and there it was. The river's elbow, or one of the many. But for us it was the one. There was space for the wind to find us here, and it licked the sweat on my neck and legs cool as I made my way down to a stretch of gravel where the river water bubbled up around the stones.

I stood, just watching the water. Time passed like in a wildlife documentary — time folded up, then stretched out to show the movement of grasses, petals, the relentless thrust of stems upwards into the light. I don't know how long we stood. But I stared so long at the river that the light falling on to the water from between the gaps of the leaves seemed to start moving on its own. I closed my eyes and thought of moths with grey-green wings stuck in a syrup of lights.

There was something that I later decided was disappointment stuck in my throat. Perhaps I was expecting a bang straight away, the envelopment of evil, something to make me believe in the stories, something to punish me and then take away my guilt.

Gravel sprayed into the river as Susumina slid down the bank beside me.

Now what? she asked. She brushed dirt from the back of my legs that had flicked up as I walked, then squeezed the leech dead without saying anything.

I sat. After a while Susumina did the same and we watched the river together, trying to see what might swim beneath our toes. The roots of trees came right down to the water here and leached their oils into it, leaving slick patches on the surface that caught rainbows in the right light. I reached to skip a stone, like it was something that I could not help doing when faced with an open space of water. But I put it back down again.

An orchid grew from a crack in a rock that jutted out from the bank. It was sheltered here; the tree above it, one that reminded me of a weeping willow but was not, hung down and let its curtain of leaves droop in the water. The orchid's roots were exposed and made their own cracks further into the rock. The stem wrapped itself around in a spiral up the roots of another plant near it. Its leaves were small, polished, and its blossoms were open, pale green-yellow. Just inside the throat of each one sat furred legs, a fleshy body. Spiders, I thought, but then I saw that they were not spiders, that the flowers were just pretending. The furred petals wobbled in the breeze. Prey or predator? I wondered what the flowers were trying to be.

I scooted down near the rock. I wanted to touch the orchid, fit its petals into the book my grandfather gave me. That way we would not come away from the river's elbow with nothing.

What are you doing? Susumina asked.

I want to take it home. Have you seen one of these before? Do you call it anything?

No. It's just a flower. No use for anything. Let's go.

Susumina watched the path now, did not let her back turn to it. The fireflies would be coming out soon. The cries of night birds would replace those of the day, and I knew Susumina wanted to hear them only from safely inside walls. So did I. I managed to dislodge the orchid with a sharp rock and, once I had retrieved it, balanced it against my hip like a child. I did not make a move to leave just yet, though. I closed my eyes.

I had thought about coming to the bend for so long and now we were here but nothing had happened except for some tricks of the light and the orchid. I had a dream about this place, but in the dream it was much deeper and damper. In the dream there was a plane here, or what we thought could be a plane. In my dream my eyes could not focus on one section of the picture at a time, and at first what I saw looked like a large dead animal lying downriver with its ribs exposed. But then I saw that the ribs were metal and the skin was the outside of the plane, peeled back in some parts.

In the dream we got closer, Susumina resisting (if this happened in reality, I think it would have been the other way around). The dream-plane had been by the river for a long time, and there must have been a fire because the inside was all black but it didn't smell like smoke. Tree roots grew through it. Scraps of vinyl here, a glint of what could be a belt buckle there. I wanted to stay and look through it, but Susumina would not stay. I've heard of this, she said. It happened a long time ago. Everyone has taken what they want from here already.

I thought people weren't allowed to come here?

Dream-Susumina shrugged.

I opened my eyes, looked at the Susumina of Real Life. She nodded back upriver. As we began to leave, something about the shadows and the cool wind made us bolt suddenly. Then we were running back the way we came, running from the bend.

As we ran I remembered the blue satin nightgown that melted, the one I hadn't wanted to pass on to my sister when it grew too small. I remembered the fantail that danced with its reflection just outside the hospital window and the nurses like a flock of birds settled on the ground below. I remembered how the sunlight pooled in the kitchen sink on the day of the funeral that I didn't go to, and the forgotten Louise cake in the fridge that eventually grew mould and had to be thrown out. And the sympathy casseroles that came afterwards. There was a counsellor with shiny silver earrings, a shiny silver pin stuck into blonde hair that was crinkled like crinkle-cut chips.

There were dreams of bones folded together, bone upon bone, in the depths of a river, air bubbles rising through the water like strings of pearls, and the white face of a girl that could have been me or it could have been Julia and it didn't matter because from fire or water, for me or Julia or my mother, I couldn't save anyone.

My sandals slipped in the leaves and rocks, and spiked vines poked at my feet, and Susumina and I gasped as if the spirits might be biting at our heels. We ran until we reached the airstrip and lay down in what was left of the grass that hadn't been burnt off by the sun.

At home I sat the orchid in one of the leftover avocado-seedling pots. My father had his radio out again. My mother paced in the kitchen.

There was no name for the orchid in the book my grandfather gave me. So, lady-in-waiting I called it. For my mother: because she was always waiting, always putting on her lipstick that no one would notice, always hiding behind her curtains, always crossing off the days on an out-of-date calendar. For Julia, because she might forever wait for me to come to the bend in the river again and rescue her, apologise, be rescued myself.

The flowers were dead by the next day, dry petals scattered. Little fake spider bodies littered all around. The orchid was no use at all in Yuvut. No good for food, no good for making houses, and no good for making decorations or medicines. No good for keeping spirits away or asking them to come closer. Just like me, it appeared where no one expected it and then vanished for no reason and no one might ever know why.

I was nervous that first night after the river, waiting for something to happen. The next day I ran to see Susumina, sure that the something must have happened to her if it had not yet happened to me. But she was fine, kicking the football against a wall and keeping her stepmother's babies out of the dirt. She laughed at my relief and made me a toy grasshopper out of a small palm frond, the kind she made her half-siblings when they were sad or hurt themselves. She did act a little more distant that day, distracted by a girl who teased her about her clothes and how she wore her hair, but I did not think much of it. After a few days I began to think that the bend in the river was our friend, that we had beaten the stories. It was safe for us, Hell for others. Until it was not.

# ORCHID
*Sorong, 1995*

*An early Dutch explorer writes: 'There is no place on earth where so many species of orchids have been found in a given area as in New Guinea. However, all this beauty is hidden away in the luxury of plant growth, and the real loveliness of these creations of this strange island continent becomes apparent only when in the hand of the collector.' He is wrong, of course, as Indra, who has just been transported along with her family from the pressing concrete of Jakarta to the wharves of Sorong, might be able to tell him. She saw the orchid she loves on her first day in Sorong, after getting off the boat. She is a transmigrasi. She is here, like so many others, because her own island is running out* of land and the government says Papua is wide and empty.

The orchid Indra loves has small red flowers, like bells. It grows by the well in the transmigrasi camp, wedged in a crook in a tree. Every day when she goes to collect water she stops and drips some water on the orchid, just a little because her mother said that orchids are best left to work towards the light on their own. That way they grow strong. Her mother would know: she remembers orchids from her own forest home on Kalimantan, back before the palm-oil plantations came and the orange smoke haze wrapped around her family's house. She remembers loving orchids, too.

The camp is near a swamp where Daud, the boy who lives next door, says he saw crocodile tracks in the mud last week. Indra does not believe him because she knows that Daud is probably just saying this to scare her, but even if he did see the tracks she doesn't care. Because this place on this island has room for breathing and running, and Daud might even teach her and her little sister to swim one day. She has been afraid of the sea, afraid of the rivers, for her whole life, but here is a chance not to be afraid any more.

The home Indra, her sister, her mother and her father left was a concrete one, in a concrete slum. There was a river nearby and it was thick and brown with rubbish. The sea was not far *away either. Some said that the land they lived on was once part of the sea anyway: reclaimed with sand and walls so that the beating noise of Jakarta could ripple further and further out, a never-ending band of concentric circles colonising what once belonged only to the sea. Indra watched her mother waiting, waiting by the door almost every day, as if she had somewhere to be. But everyone's walls pressed closer and closer, and there was nowhere to go. Next door, in a concrete house just like theirs, Indra's neighbour drew bad pictures to sell at night and winked through the curtains at her during the day.*

*Indra's mother taught her about the sea goddesses who take children, especially boys, away. Which is why I have no sons, she said, but never explained any more than this. So Indra never went close to the sea in their old home. But she sees it here often. Her father has built a shop with thin triplex walls down by the beach, and sells food and fuel to the fishermen. He likes to sell coconuts best because they remind him of the home that Indra did not get to see, the one on Kalimantan, before Jakarta, where he met Indra's mother and used to have what they now come to Papua seeking: room to sell, room to live, room to breathe. Indra goes down to the shop in the evenings, after school, and helps him clean up the coconut scraps from the day. When they are finished, they sit together, sucking the last of the white flesh from the young green coconuts, and watch the fishermen returning home.*

*Two weeks ago, Indra's mother caught malaria here, but lived, and the house they have just built is thin wood with a roof that rattles so loud in the rain that nothing else can be heard. It leaks, they have to go to the bathroom outside, and it takes weeks for mail to arrive from their past homes. But Indra loves the orchid by the well, and she is going to learn how to swim, and her father has his coconuts, her little sister climbed a tree yesterday, and her mother remembers again what it feels like to stand by a window and look out as far as she can see.*

## TWENTY-EIGHT

This is what happened the last time I saw Susumina.

Want to go do something? Go to the elbow? I asked her on the airstrip, half teasing. The airstrip was losing its grass to the drought and contractors were slowly covering it, from the top to the bottom, with limestone gravel from the mountains.

No time, said Susumina. I have to help Grandma.

Later, then?

I have other things to do. I'm getting older, you know.

We had still played together after that time at the river's elbow, but it was true that she joined the football games on the airstrip less and less these days. She was spending lots of time talking to her grandmother, stepmother and aunts, and had even started creating her own bag out of string when she sat down at the pasar. Her grandmother bought her new clothes and I saw her showing them off to her cousins, instead of me. I felt a shifting in my chest, like I had grabbed for something and only grasped air. I talked too quickly, too much like a little child, just to fill the spaces that seemed to grow between us.

But what about Ronaldo?

Ronaldo is never coming here and I am never going where he is. I am becoming a woman.

So am I, I said, thinking of a moment earlier when I was shirtless because of the heat and suddenly I noticed the air on my nipples as though I had never noticed them before.

Not the same, said Susumina. Where is your garden?

She hefted a bag of sweet potatoes up on her head. She smelled different lately. Like the pig fat that the older kids smeared themselves with on nights when they danced and their songs travelled through the darkness to our house where I lay awake.

I stuck my tongue out at her, as if we were being silly, but she did not smile back.

See you later then, I said.

Mmm, she said and walked off.

From behind I saw that her hips had widened and children ran up to her as if they trusted her. From behind I could imagine her as someone else one day, someone I did not know any more. And that's the last I saw of her. But I thought it was just going to be a few hours, a few days, until I saw her running back up to our house, football tucked under her arm, skirt whipping around her legs.

---

El Niño got larger. There were stories of frosts further up in the highlands where they never were before, turning sweet potato leaves brown, killing bananas in their skins, turning taro bad in the earth. People across Papua set fields alight, because there was a rumour that the clouds of smoke from the fires would turn into rain clouds and bring relief. Every day we woke up to haze that got deeper and deeper. At first it just yellowed the edges of the day. Then it thickened and made the world sunset. On the days before my parents decided to pack up and leave until the rains came, the haze made us all swim in amber syrup. It made its way into the house, making us all wheeze. Several of the old people and babies died within days of each other, coughing as their family members tried in vain to keep the haze from finding its way into their homes, through every crack.

The hospital, despite everything, perhaps hearing my mother's growing desperation, was growing out of the cracked clay, though its progress was slow. One day it was all bare bones and spaces, and the next there were some empty rooms. Then shelves that would one day hold medicines. Someone in Australia donated one of those special incubators for keeping premature babies alive. It sat in the tool shed by the hospital, empty and useless with no power source. Basically a giant paperweight, said Dad. But what could he tell the donors? It just showed up.

But that incubator was not what was really on Dad's mind. More riots came to Indonesia's cities. The pilots had nothing else to talk about. Part of me wanted to be there. To see the bullets and cars on fire for myself. As if they might make me feel like I was doing something, that this was my place, too, though my lighter hair was still lucky to the newly arrived Javanese and Sulawesi women quietly setting up shops along the airstrip, who covered their own hair with polyester spangled with sequins. They called the people of Yuvut dirty because of the colour of their skin, and bolted their doors against them with two or more locks at night. The people of Yuvut bought their cooking oil, their beanies and their rubber sandals from the Sulawesi women, and kept on watching the skies for rain that did not come. The haze got thicker, the air got drier and drier so that my hair stood up in wisps, and everything metal zapped in the mornings.

And then a pilot came and my father talked to him and we had one hour to pack before the pilot came back and took us away. Because there was no water in the rain tanks, the swamp was too thick with roots and pig muck, and the creek was muddied with the needs of too many people with too many buckets. As I climbed into the plane, I looked out the window and there was no Susumina to wave to. Leavings always seem drawn out in movies, with plenty of time for goodbyes, but sometimes that is not what really happens. We got to leave: the pilot, my mother, my father and I. We got to leave with our one bag each, with my one bear (I chose Patches, out of sympathy), a few clothes, toothbrushes. We left for the city where there would be water in trucks for those who needed it and toilets that flushed more often than not.

I wondered what the people of Yuvut would do while we were gone. Many of the government workers from elsewhere, and the contractors from the other islands who worked on government buildings and other projects, were leaving, too. One family at least every day lined up on the airstrip with their boxes and backpacks, until the people of Yuvut could have it back for themselves. But we from Elsewhere had run the place almost dry, even parts of the river.

As the plane taxied down the airstrip I imagined I saw Susumina waiting by a stand of bananas at the far end where we often sat to watch the wheels of the planes rush over our heads. As we flew up, I saw the river, no longer green but brown and white with exposed rocks like it was signalling for help from the sky. I tried to see the bend but we were too quickly turning and leaving all that behind. Out we flew from our place in between the mountains, and then the sky seemed to open up through the haze and be large again.

I heard the pilot yell out over the engine. Down below, he said, there were inland beaches of white sand over black rocks, and underneath your feet the endless echo of underground caves whose entrances could never be reached. I knew from other pilots that there were places where oil seeped out of the earth, fields of natural gas that might burn for decades. There were mountains that rose high in fog, and were marked off for the military, where civilians could never go. All this was supposed to be below me, but what I could see were trees, cracks in mountain peaks, and that haze of dust and smoke that poured from the mountains and ate its way through the lowland plains all the way to the sea. But I could imagine everything: the glaciers that once spanned miles and were shrinking too fast, the sandalwood forests falling like wheat under foreign chainsaws, the giant hydroelectric plant that was supposed one day to be Papua's beating heart. I imagined, too, the tinier forms of life, the dancing birds of paradise, the spirits waiting at the edge of things for their time to come, waiting for the water to get low enough in the swamps and expose all of Papua's hidden secrets: its bodies of planes, of people. Its quicksand, its mountain violets. Its things that sound impossible or like they should never be seen together. Birds with ribbons for tails. Kangaroos and people living in trees. Mammals that can fly. Alpine orchids, snowcaps right next to jungle vines.

Susumina told me once that some of the old men of Yuvut, who had never flown, asked the young people who had flown if they saw God up there in the clouds. And the young people said there was no God because they never saw him while they were in the planes. And they asked me about astronauts and I said that I didn't know if they had seen God either.

## TWENTY-NINE

Sentani was a place of more smoke. We could not get away from it. From the grills of the street carts, the cooking fires by the lake's edge, burning rubbish spilling into a river (an aerosol can exploding every now and then). From the men's cigarettes as they passed on motorbikes, from the engines of broken quarry trucks roasting in the sun. From the fireworks that went off whenever I was not expecting it, like gunshots in a crowded street.

The riots for Papuan independence were simmering. Not gone, just a pot on slow boil. The feelings of them could still be felt rumbling through words thrown between drunks and punches felt from boys made invincible on the fumes of glue and paint. The rioters still wanted the Indonesian government out of Papua. They wished especially that the police and soldiers would leave. But they also understood that sometimes one has so many disappointments that one has to hope for smaller things at first — like vanished guerrillas returned (even if just their bodies), like the chance to elect government representatives who look like them and will not be assassinated or bought.

In the city, foreigners had worked very hard to make places where they could escape the smoke and the people. Such as the school for missionary children perched high on the hill, and where people could sell American candy on sports days and, were it not for the heat, they could close their eyes and imagine themselves home again. Which, for them, was usually America.

We were not the only foreign family lifted out of a Papuan village that week, or the last. Every day more families arrived from the far edges of Papua, the dryness forcing everyone to Sentani's lake like tadpoles gathering in a shrinking pool. We were all installed in places around the town, but mostly on another hill, next to the school hill, where there were curved concrete bunkers left over from the American military and the Second World War days. We moved into those bunkers and other concrete houses, settled in as if for a siege. How long are we going to stay here? I asked my parents.

Until the rains come. Until the riots stop. Until the soldiers aren't so quick on their triggers. They did not tell me that last part in so many words.

Mum stood by the curtains in Sentani just like she did in Yuvut and I knew she was still counting down on some calendar somewhere, even if that countdown never had a real endpoint.

I met a policeman on the street while I bought fruit from a cart. I asked him about the school on the hill, because my parents were going to send me there to give Mum a break from home school.

Ghosts live up there, the policeman told me. Ghosts guard the way to the school. He shivered and continued — I saw one when it was raining one day.

I can't go to that school, Mum, I said while she laid clothes on the bed for my first day. A shirt with a collar that I would swap for a tee-shirt. A skirt that might make way for jeans.

Mmm, she said.

Ghosts live there.

Even if they do, she said, you're going anyway.

I went, smelling like my mother's perfume that I splashed on my armpits because I suddenly realised that I had a scent and that I was growing.

The school was all clean concrete and wooden lockers. Mown grass and lunches delivered hot, wrapped in brown paper. This was how the expat children, with patchworked accents and bodies straining against American clothes that no longer fitted, included their chillies and rice in between classes on all-white presidents and how to write cheques before they became obsolete.

Alyssa was one of these Americans. Alyssa was short, with a chest already growing that she tried to hide because the school rulebook specifically pointed out chests as something to be hidden, though she got into trouble for it anyway. She was from Georgia. The state, not the country. She got straight As, sang in the worship band and was the teacher's favourite in Bible class. She also liked to steal. Useless things, mainly. Like toilet paper, a banana, light bulbs. But I found out all of this later.

I was in my first class, maths, when she sat next to me. Hi, she said. Have a Coke.

I took the Coke. Alyssa didn't need translations of my speech, even though it still clung to its flat-vowelled New Zealand roots. In the next class, she cleared a space next to her and said to a boy, No, that's Ruth's spot. You can't sit there.

She translated me for everyone in English class when I tried to talk about *The Secret Garden* and the teacher said, I just love your accent.

After school we lay on our backs in the grass of the football field (illegally because the army had a gun range in the gully directly below us, and the principal just announced, Children, the army is practising again. Please keep off the field and other outdoor areas). It was not unheard-of for bullets to ricochet off the gym wall. They had only ever hit one person, and it was non-fatal. We were invincible, anyway. It was easy to feel that way when you saw Papua's dead and dying too often. Because if you did not feel invincible, then all you felt was fear. Not that we had the language for that then.

Do you like it here? I asked Alyssa.

Of course, she said. But the key to liking it is to know that it is a good place *and* a bad place, too. Like anywhere else, I guess. You'll get in trouble for how your clothes look sometimes, but they'll also remember your birthday and they make really good cakes.

I smiled. *Here*, I thought. This is the place where I can make myself clean.

The space where my spleen was (if I were to believe Susumina's story) had stopped feeling so empty while I was with Susumina. It had opened up for aches and wishes, some shiftings that some days felt like hope and other days felt like pain. After the dengue fever I was not always sure when a moment of faintness (when the whole world seemed to be speeding away from me in a tunnel while I stood deaf, sweating) was an after-effect of that illness or a thought of Julia. But here without Susumina, in the sounds and movement of Sentani, I was able to lock those feelings back, to tell myself that Ruth, not Ru, was a single daughter with few griefs. Here, for a short time, numbness could feel like healing.

The pool on the hill where we stayed used to be electric blue but had faded and turned greenish with scum. It seemed strange to swim in a pool in the middle of a drought. But this is where we (the families plucked from the interior) spent many of our afternoons and weekends as we waited for the rains to come. It was as if the only feeling that felt right was the one that came when suspended midway in the air between the diving board and the deep end of the pool.

I feel like we should have stayed, said a Canadian mother to my mum. How come we get to go and they don't?

Some can leave, said another. German, this time, with hair of impossible straightness in Sentani's heat. There is money floating around.

Yes, said the first mother. But not all. And something doesn't feel quite right.

I wrapped my towel around my damp shoulders and watched one of the missionary kid boys, about the same age as me, show his friend a bullet casing from his pocket. I collect them, he said. Machine-gun belt clips, bullet casings, sometimes even the whole bullets. They're all left over from World War Two and other things.

His friend turned the casing, a dull copper, in the sunlight. These missionary kids were alike in many ways. They were the kind that jumped as high as they could from steep cliffs into unknown water below. They were the kind that, when they were older, rode motorbikes down the Sentani airstrip, daring someone to catch them. When I first heard the word 'missionary' I had very different pictures in my head of what they would be like: long-dressed, long-haired, Bible always in their hands, looking down from their Heaven perches. Papua was one of their favourite campgrounds, but we were as close as you got in Yuvut. Other villages might have one or two missionary families but the cities were a different story.

And some of them *were* long-haired and pious. There were large families wearing matching prints, and six-inch rules in between high-school couples. There were people who corrected my father at Bible Study and shook their heads when Mum sent me outside in too-short shorts. But some of them were not like that. There was a woman who brought my mother cupcakes made out of real butter, not the usual Blueband margarine that even ants would not eat. There was the woman who asked my mother to play hockey at school, even though Mum always said no while she watched from the sidelines. There was the man who knew how to fix the borrowed motorbike when it made Dad swear, and he did it all for free.

Friendships among the Sentani expats formed, based on connections as thin and strong as cocoon silk. Sometimes on weekends I was Alyssa's lookout as she snuck bags of chips and peppermint candies out of shops under her skirt. Everyone knew that someone could get snatched away at any second. Pilots died, people might get cancer and diabetes and leave the island forever, relatives back home needed help, babies had to be born, families were broken. This was why, I think, we lay on football fields in range of ricocheting bullets, why high-schoolers did not check the water below them before jumping, why many, as young as fourteen, rode their motorbikes with no helmets. And all of us, while we waited and waited for the rains to come, met around the swimming pool that made us guilty, and ate American candy so that we could imagine we were not really there.

Alyssa and I liked the deep end of the pool best. Her mother let us drop an old bracelet in and dive for it all the way down. At the bottom of the pool, I watched other swimming shapes above me, their voices and splashes muffled, guessing at who they were and wondering about things like leaving and staying, and the problems of being the one who is always watching, like the world has been flattened and fitted onto my own TV screen.

Sometimes, when the heat and smoke became even more dense, so that a cough settled into the bottom of our lungs and became an old friend, we rode in the neighbour's car up to a higher hill, where there was more wind coming in from the sea. There was a tall white cross on the otherwise bare hill, and sometimes there were offerings at its base. A wooden bead, a photo of a young woman. An eggcup, sweet-potato chips arranged in a heart. The school decided to hold a dawn prayer meeting there one day, to pray for rain. We pressed with our bodies around the cross, while the wind tore our words from our lips before they could be heard, and carried them off in every direction towards the city and the mountains and the sea: everywhere but up. The prayers mixed with the dust and smoke and our waiting thickened.

## BANANA
*Unmapped swamp, 1944*

Kota Mori is dying and he knows this. He is only seventeen but he knows what dying is. When he was first sent to New Guinea, uniform crisp, mother proud, he shuddered every time he heard of a plane going down in the trees, in the mountains. Every time his reaction felt the same: the ripple in his stomach, the scent of vomit in his nostrils. The vision of skin and metal on fire. But planes kept going down and pilots and passengers kept dying and the stories of their deaths became familiar. (He recorded all his fears in a journal that, like most journals, remains inconclusive and open to interpretation.)

Above Kota's head is a banana flower. Its burgundy bleeds purple from its thick stem *hanging from the banana tree, and its tightly packed petals are just starting to split and show the yellowish brood of florets underneath. Hanging there, right above Kota, it looks like someone's heart suspended in the air, darkly red and pulsing in the breeze. As Kota breathes (his breaths are getting harder and slower) he can smell the banana tree's sap where someone's bullet sliced through it. Flies, midges are thick around the sap and thick around the blood pooling under Kota's back. He supposes that he does prefer to die this way: with a bullet. It's supposed to be less frightening than a plane crash. He isn't sure where he got that idea from, though. He thinks dying this way might also be less frightening than dying the way he heard some of his fellow soldiers died not so far away, on an island called Biak, riddled with caves. The caves were a blessing, at first. They let the Japanese soldiers hole up in them like rabbits. They did not see sunlight for weeks, but they were alive and they had supplies to last them. But, like rabbits, they could be smoked out. The smoking out took the form of dynamite and diesel fuel on fire. Caves can only go so deep, men can only run so fast.*

*One of his friends in his regiment, Haruki, cooked with banana blossom once. He said he got the recipe from a young woman in Thailand, where he was stationed previously. 'Sure it was a young woman?' Kota said, teasing him. 'I bet it was actually an old lonely woman.'* Haruki laughed and kept on with his cooking. He gently pulled out every pistil from the florets, because they are the tough and flavourless parts, and then peeled back the outside of every floret that he had collected from just outside camp. He soaked the florets overnight, to remove bitterness. He and the rest of the men were tired of bitterness. They had enough of it already in their malaria treatments that happened too frequently.

Underneath all the dark outer petals of the main part of the banana flower, its core is yellow-white and tender. Haruki sliced it, mixed it with the florets, and cooked them into a curry with coconut and lime, chilli paste and herbs. When they ate it, it tasted to Kota like it was alive and dancing.

He was excited to step off his ship onto New Guinea soil. Excited to see what his gun could do for the first time, and excited to get off a ship on the sea that had made him seasick most of the time. He imagined flower-perfumed air and birds flashing in the trees like jewels. For some reason he did not imagine the people, thinking instead that the Papuan forest was empty, perfectly suited to a game of war. There really were birds like jewels and there were also flowers. But there were also mosquitoes and leeches that made him feel like he could not help forever bleeding dry. There was mud. Every day, more mud, until even at night he could *not shake the feeling of sinking, sinking, heavy weights on legs that were never going to take him anywhere. And always the sting and the stick of sweat on grass-whipped shins, the small sores that blossomed in hours into pus-filled ulcers in the heat and damp. And he couldn't escape the people either, who made him feel as if he were intruding at a private event and he must apologise.*

*Last night Haruki did not come back from his scouting trip out by the northern edges of their current swamp. Kota took his place today and found out why Haruki did not come back. One night when they first arrived, and still had the sea's winds to blow away biting insects, Haruki and Kota sat with their feet in the water and lay back to watch the sky, daring the Australians, the Americans and anyone else to see them. 'You know what?' said Haruki. 'We're all just on the edge of something called madness. We're all just sitting with our toes dipped in that dark water and the only thing separating mad from not mad is how far we let ourselves slip in.'*

*Kota, as the bullet (American? Australian? Neither?) takes his life, turns from the banana flower and stares into the dead eyes of Haruki lying close to him, and imagines they are back together at camp, spooning banana-blossom curry into their mouths and guessing the names of foreign stars.*

# THIRTY

*Miriam.* Too long in a village backwater that doesn't appear on most maps. Too long mothering an only child who should have been the elder of two. I have a letter from my mother, saying that she and my father have moved into a nursing home where she can grow begonias on the windowsill and they serve sticky date pudding every Friday.

*Ruth.* When we go back to New Zealand I do not think it will be the same place I remember from Julia days. I remember standing in a supermarket, looking at all the toothpastes we could choose from. After being in Yuvut, the air in New Zealand will seem as if all the smells are sucked out and replaced with air that does not even feel like it is really there, except for the fact that we are breathing it. Like air from a diver's tank or from a dying patient's respirator. It will be too clean.

*Miriam.* Rose sent me a photo of Julia's grave while we were in

Sentani. The cherry tree we planted had died and someone had replaced it with a gardenia. The blooms were starting to split. In a Chinese-Indonesian restaurant, with Disney characters on the walls, there was a TV and we saw blurred footage on the one English channel that told of riots in the mountains behind us.

*Ruth.* Tensions have risen, said the newscaster with a tie too tight and who pronounced the names all wrong. His mouth took away the bodies of people and replaced them with brackets full of numbers and dates. When we left Yuvut, perhaps Susumina was angry and that is why she didn't come to the airstrip to say goodbye. We are all so angry, but maybe we do not even know why.

*Susumina.* I took the calendar with the crosses on the squares from Ruth's family kitchen while they were gone. I took a lollipop as well, but spat it out halfway through. I am now too old for lollipops.

*Miriam.* For those we left behind (in New Zealand, in Yuvut) it is as if we have stood still in time, and over the oceans they still send me the words that can be found gilded and stamped in sympathy cards. As for me, I can collapse the experience of years and of others like an accordion. Isn't that what the old people do? So much happens in so short a space that it needs to be reduced to nothing so that we can wrap our hands around it and throw it away or hoard it close.

*Ruth.* My memories of Julia get chewed around the edges. I find myself trying to picture her face without hunting for the photo album that Mum keeps in her underwear drawer, buried under the bras and sleeping pills. Here is a newspaper clipping from the day Julia died: Local child burned in household fire dies from complications associated with her injuries. The police remind the public that this is a warning to parents to constantly supervise children around fireplaces and other household hazards. A service will be held at 2 p.m. at 50 Starveal Street.

*Miriam.* My mother saved her obituary. *Julia Rose Glass. 18 Jan. 1992–30 Apr. 1997. Loved daughter, sister and granddaughter. Gone too soon.* You can't blame yourself, said Rose. Don't all mothers blame themselves? I said. I am still not forgiven.

*Ruth.* In moving pictures every day. Tornado kills whole family. Factory collapse kills hundreds. Mine explosion kills twelve. How horrible, we say, and shake our heads. And then we forget. I stood over Julia's grave before we left and I was afraid because I was forgetting and I knew there was still more to forget. I'm sorry, I said again. It felt like the right thing to say, but I still do not know how to feel forgiven or to forgive.

# THIRTY-ONE

When I visited Julia, that one time after the accident, the hospital room smelled of soap and cornflakes, sweet milk and steel. The walls were white, so white, and seemed to pulse with the beep of the monitors attached by cords to Julia, with the drip of the IV. Under the bandages, all I could see of her was her lips. Somehow unscarred, but pressed and puffed. Someone had tied a pink balloon to the end of the bed. Julia hated pink. The IV dripped. Clear beads chasing themselves into her veins. And there was that fantail at the window.

I felt as if I should introduce myself first before trying to take her hand. Dry fingertips peeped out from bandages and dream-soft gauze.

Instead I told her that I would tell her a story: the Jorinda and Joringel one that she loved. Only, I left the book at home, so this time I told it from my head.

The IV dripped.

*Once upon a time there lived two sisters called Jorinda and Joringel. Joringel got a boy's name because her father was hoping for a boy when she was born but he didn't get his wish.*

*The sisters lived near a huge forest where they liked to play. In the middle of this forest was a big castle made of glass. The castle was owned by an old woman who was lonely and sad. Some called her a witch because it was said that she could turn herself into any shape she chose. But most often a cat or a bird, depending on whether she was chasing or being chased. And it was also said that she captured young girls who strayed too near her castle. Probably because she was so sad and so lonely.*

*One day, the two sisters accidentally got too close to the castle. Jorinda was singing, but then her song changed and she was turned into a nightingale. Joringel could do nothing because suddenly she was paralysed and her legs felt like concrete in water. And then the old woman came and snatched up Jorinda and put her in a cage to take to her castle. It was only after they disappeared that Joringel could move again. And then it was too late. Jorinda was gone.*

The IV dripped. My mother came into the room. Her hair was loose in the way it was only when she first got up in the morning. Usually she had it twisted tight behind her head. My father sat in a chair near Julia, shifting and flipping too fast through a year-old tabloid magazine so that he had to keep turning back the pages. There were antibacterial handwipes For Visitors' Use everywhere. Miriam handed me one now.

Time to go home, Ruth, said Mum.

But I haven't finished telling her the story, I said. What I did not say: What if she is dead before we get to the end? Then what happens?

Time to go, said my mother.

My father stayed behind with Julia, examining the numbers on the machine by her side and muttering something about levels and checks. As we left, I could hear the fantail tap-tap-tapping at the window, trying to break through its reflection to meet its own self head first.

At home, I put the kettle on to make tea for my mother. The kettle we had then was electric with a clear body so I could watch the bubbles rise and wrestle at the surface.

You don't have to do that, Ruth, she said. It's too heavy when it's full.

I want to, I said.

Mum let me have hot chocolate out of the Christmas tin and we took our drinks to the back porch, even though it was chilly.

I used to tell you stories, she said. Didn't I?

Yes, I said.

She held my hand, which made me stiff at first, remembering Julia and the flames, until she rubbed my palm with hers, warming my fingers and letting a small part of myself unravel. We shivered in the wind, watching the cars on the highway just beyond the apple orchard. Somewhere a leaf blower was blowing; somewhere else there was the high cry of a hawk.

My mum, said Miriam, didn't really tell me many stories, though I know she tells them to you and Julia now.

I squeezed her fingers, feeling like she was about to take them away. But she did not.

Now, in Sentani, when the evening cooled the concrete over the septic tank enough to lie on it, Alyssa and I told each other stories and peeled fleshy rambutans out of their tight skins until the mosquitoes chased us back inside. The aching call to prayer from the mosque down the road shivered through the air — a sound I loved because it sounded like someone searching, someone asking. Someone looking for home.

Alyssa had a story she learned from her Hindu nanny while her parents went to language school in Bandung, on the island of Java:

In the beginning, there was a god called Batara Guru, with a beautiful wife called Dewi Uma. One day, he got his wife pregnant even though she did not want to have a baby. The baby became the god of the underworld, Batara Kala. He is a rude god, and always hungry, and what he wants to eat are the children who are created when their mothers don't want them to be, or are born to mothers but have no fathers. Batara Kala is also the god of time. His speciality is finding those who are unlucky: wrong place, wrong time. He waits for the unlucky and consumes them whole. Some people are just born into unluckiness, feet first instead of head first. When that happens, there are ways to try to keep Batara Kala away and keep the child safe. But it must be done quickly, and it must be done right. On days when the moon gets between the earth and the sun, or when the moon falls into the earth's shadow, that is when Batara Kala is especially hungry: so hungry that he leaves the earth and chases the sun and moon to fill his belly. But the sun and the moon are too strong and he will forever be chasing them, forever not full.

# THIRTY-TWO

After two months of waiting by the pool in Sentani, the rains came. They came heavy. The soil could not hold their heaviness, and bridges and homes were washed away. Alyssa and I danced in the mud with the children who played chicken with the cars on our street. Worms and beetles surfaced everywhere. Frog song drowned out birdsong. The mosquitoes became too thick to spend our evenings outside. Down in the main area of town, the body of a cow got stuck under a broken bridge. On the first day it folded into the side of the stream, deflated. On the second day it had bloated large again. The bridge was in two pieces: one tilted toward the sky, and the other slipped underneath it towards the water that would not stop. Concrete and steel splintered everywhere. The rain did not stop. People needed to get from one side of the bridge to the other. Someone laid layers of plywood planks across what was left of the bridge.

Holding hands, holding umbrellas, people walked across. A lone brave motorcycle tested it, succeeded. More followed his example, hitting the planks fast so that they barely seemed to touch them.

On the night of day three, Dad and I waited for our turn to cross the bridge after going to the other side to pick up cereal, rice, powdered milk. Sentani was so hot that the shops closed every day for part of the afternoon, making dusk the time when everyone rushed to buy. Dad bought us ice creams. The power to the supermarket's freezer turned off and on so often that the ice cream had melted and refrozen just as many times. Its sugar had crystallised like stalactites. We sucked our ice creams and watched the steam rise from the road and the bridge under the streetlights in the steady drizzle. A wall of sound rose from the other side. Men started pushing through, not waiting their turn. Then more men came behind them, carrying a long lacquered black box on their shoulders. It's a coffin, Dad said to me, but I barely heard him through the people and the rain and the river. I looked down at the cow beneath the bridge. It was still bloated, but a dog or something else had got at it in the night and torn at its stomach. A veil of bugs gathered at its eyes and wounds.

When the others waiting to cross saw the men with the coffin, they parted, clearing the path to the bridge. Shopping was not the only thing that could wait until evening sometimes. Funerals, too, were easier once the day's heat had passed. As the pallbearers crossed, the planks that weren't touching any part of the existing concrete bridge bowed and creaked. People on both sides of the bridge yelled at the men, fearing for them. But the men crossing ignored them. They walked heavy and quick. Their shirts were soaked. They wore their good funeral clothes, which now became see-through in some places. They raised the coffin high in the air, perhaps out of instinct, when they were at the midpoint of their crossing. And then they were over and the crowd on our side surged forward, pulling them onwards and sending them on their way down the road.

The people on our side of the bridge had waited a long time to cross. People grumbled and shuffled, checked on their children. But once the coffin was through, it seemed to be our turn. We lined up. But the press of people behind us, the pushing hands, made us all fall, together, too close to the bridge's edge where everything threatened to crumble away.

Hold my shirt, said Dad. Hold it. Don't let go.

We were almost at the beginning of the planks, almost ready to cross. Then the electricity turned off again and the streetlights went dark. There was nothing to see at first but the light of a couple of digital watch faces and cigarette butts floating in the gloom. I was still holding onto Dad's shirt. But he had become a shadow and I was a shadow and all the shadows around us pushed us on while pulling us apart at the same time. I looked up. There was a gap in the rain clouds and through it I could see the stars, thick and close. I stumbled. I lost Dad's shirt. But my feet did not stop moving and someone in the dark grabbed my collar and pulled me along the bridge. Perhaps I should have been afraid. But I was not afraid. I let myself be pulled and pressed. Then the hand on the back of my collar let go. I stood still for a second, feeling the constant brushing of bodies moving past. Then the lights came back on.

Ruth! called Dad, from the side of the road. Someone beside me saw him call to me, and grabbed my hand, taking me back to my father's side before melting back into the sweep of bodies rushing past.

Dad hugged me to him. He brushed my hair out of my eyes. Well, that was something, he said.

Somewhere I lost my ice cream. I'll get you another tomorrow, Dad said. His eyes looked large in the night but he was not afraid, he was smiling. He did not seem to mind the bodies brushing by him as he might have another time. He let us be carried along with them. We walked back to the bottom of our hill and caught a motorcycle-taxi up. I sat on the back, both of us with no helmets. I held on tight to his waist and could feel the way he moved with the motorcycle. Like he had done it before, like he knew what he was doing.

## ALPINE GRASSES
*Mount Carstensz, 2016*

*Agus, Budi and Soni are new recruits and newly posted to secure the area around the Mountain Mine. This means that Yoes, one of the older guards, takes it upon himself to tell them about the mountain's ghost. The days are boring if you are posted high on the mountain, and the nights can be more so. Agus and Budi are from Java, but Soni is from Papua, though far from this mountain, and he is eager to fit in, eager to make friends with this group, so he urges Yoes on as they all sit in the thin grass, sucking pieces of it between their teeth.*

*The ghost is a Dutch nurse who (at first) survived the crash that killed everyone else aboard her flight in the latter part of the Second*

World War. The crash should have killed her. But the rough diary she kept on the remains of the plane's safety card and the inside of one of its doors tell history that she survived. The plane's body shattered over the mountain's high rocks like glass. But the nurse did not die yet. She broke bones, had wounds that got infected but, because of the altitude, did not fester as quickly as she knew they would if the plane had crashed lower down the mountain.

They crashed below the summit of Puncak Jaya. It was not just bare rock, even though it was above the treeline. The Dutch nurse found herself surrounded by stiff tussock-like grasses. They reminded her of a field trip to Switzerland when she was a girl and the meadow grasses there (this part is not provided in the diary, but offered by one of Yoes's friends who has been to Switzerland and seen such scenes). She packed her wounds with their blades and was grateful for them then, but not later when she found them impossible to chew and swallow. They had no nutritional value to her, only to the tiny butterflies that surprised her one particularly sunny morning.

With her wounds she could not go far. She kept her diary for a few days, remembering stories of other crash survivors who had done the same thing, but that did not keep her alive either. In the end, it was simple starvation that took her. Once she was dead, though, she found *herself free from her wounds to move about the mountain. Then she was able to see all the other bodies the mountain had claimed, and all the ones that it was still to claim. It was quiet there on the mountain for years. She saw planes flying overhead and prayed no more of them would crash. She saw Papuan hunting parties tracking pigs and birds further down the mountain. She saw when the Indonesian soldiers came and how badly the Papuans wanted to keep their land. There were a few Western explorers and scientists. Mainly botanists and geologists. It was the geologists whom she watched most carefully because she already knew what they were going to find in her mountain. She had seen the green veins that meant copper even before she died. And she knew of the gold, too.*

*When the mining operations began, she followed the tunnels deeper into her mountain. She liked listening to the men at work and sat with her favourites as they ate their lunches. But now their machines are still eating deeper and deeper into the rock. The Indonesian soldiers are here to stay and so are the miners who come from everywhere around the world. (Yoes looks at Soni, and Agus and Budi shift in their positions.) Australians, Russians, even some Dutch. Listening to her own language must have given the nurse a thrill for a few weeks.*

*Yoes leaves the story there, letting Agus, Budi and Soni imagine the ghost for themselves and scare themselves later when they hear things that are not there. Soni continues the story in his head —*

The miners are carving out Papua's heart and leaving it hollow. He is happy he got this job. It is a good job, good money, and so far not much work. He does not know and is not related to the Papuans who live around the mountain. But still, he thinks, the Dutch nurse might have celebrated the activity of the miners at first. She liked the company. But the mountain is becoming all mud and gravel, and the Dutch nurse worries that the gold and copper will turn everything it touches gold and dead, like the Midas story she read about in school. The copper and gold have to run out at some point. And then her mountain will return to its quiet. That's why she spends her time on the lower levels of the mine now, watching and waiting for the deep rich veins to run dry. When they do, she thinks, then she will return to the mountain top. But, as the men dig deeper and deeper with their machines, she thinks of the types of wounds that never heal, and the ones that must be mortal.

# THIRTY-THREE

The rains meant it was time to go back to Yuvut, time for Dad to make one last push for the hospital. If Mum was unhappy about this, she did not say so out loud. Since coming to Sentani, she had stopped asking about the hospital out loud and instead prayed and prayed for the rains, knowing that their coming meant the hospital might have an endpoint, and that meant one day she might step into a plane that would take her away from this island. She had changed in this way; Dad was no longer cradling his radios; and perhaps (I hoped) I might have changed in some way, too. Maybe Dad was right about this year.

So Mum counted and recounted the supplies we needed to bring with us to Yuvut: six boxes of noodles, two cases of Sprite, one case of Coca-Cola. Only three jars of spaghetti sauce (because it was heavy and expensive, and this was all that was on the supermarket shelves when we stocked up). More toilet paper than Dad thought we needed, because you never know. One jar of peanut butter that she was already telling me to be sparing with. Sacks of rice, flour, sugar. Two trays of eggs, tied up with the plastic pink *talis* string. Four precious soup-powder packets sent from New Zealand that took months to arrive. Mum would use them to flavour stews. To get them, Dad and I had to travel to the post office in Jayapura, an hour's drive from Sentani, because mail had slowed to a trickle in recent weeks and the rumour was that the post office manager in Jayapura was holding back foreigners' mail on purpose. Why? I asked Dad. Money reasons, unhappiness reasons. It was standard that mail from 'outside' took about two months to arrive. But now some people never got their mail at all. One family got their chocolate advent calendar over a year late. It had been chewed by rats and melted and remelted too many times. Other families got their packages but things were missing. Magazines and marshmallows were especially good at vanishing.

Probably ants, said the mailman at the Sentani office. People should be more careful.

On the way to Jayapura, the car we borrowed wound through the lakeside hills. I counted landslides on the hills, and the trucks below them carving out their hearts. I became sick with the smells of petrol and paint, hot road and open sewers. Then we made a turn and Jayapura was below us, with its square-roofed buildings stacked on each other and eating into more hillsides. The post office in Jayapura was a long building near the port, lined with windows without panes or screens. Outside the front door was a shipment of schoolbooks in broken wooden crates. Pages of maths problems lay disintegrating in the mud. A chicken pecked through them.

The post office manager is not in, said a man sitting on the building's front stoop, chewing betel.

Can I look through for my packages? asked Dad, waving towards the piles of dust-covered parcels just visible behind him. The man shrugged, rearranged his waistband and moved aside so we could go in.

We went to where the bulk of the personal packages seemed to be piled, separate from the shipments for businesses. We saw many familiar last names. Dad wrote them down so that he could pass on the information to some of the Americans, Koreans, Germans and Australians back in Sentani who were waiting for their mail, too. We saw a package with a stamp from nine months ago, addressed to a family who had to return to Canada last month because the mother went to Singapore where the doctors saw she had cancer, stage four. She never came back to Sentani to pack up her house. She was gone, and then her family was gone, one suitcase each. Just like that. Some of their friends held a garage sale for their things. Dad got tools, Mum got tea towels with pictures of US states on them, and I got a Polly Pocket with only one piece missing.

We were lucky at the post office. Dad found the package with the soups from New Zealand after about thirty minutes. George and Rose had sent it, along with a pair of bottle-green leggings that were too small for me, some deodorant for Mum that wouldn't make her armpits sting like the Indonesian ones did, and a packet of dried peas that the rats had got partway into. We also found a letter from my parents' church with a card for Easter, long passed, and three chocolate eggs. Or what used to be chocolate eggs, anyway.

We took our mail and went to the supermarket nearby that sometimes had more on its shelves than the Sentani ones. Mum had given us a list that morning. There is a smell that all supermarkets in Indonesia have: shrimp paste and dust, laundry powder and (often) the sweet-sick of durian. We stood in the aisles for a minute. It's hard to think in terms of months, said Dad. I looked at him, quickly. I could not guess any more how much time he was going to spend on the hospital, and for a minute I felt like I could know what my mother felt. I saw a shampoo that I had once seen in New Zealand. Something like another memory shot through me, but with no real shape.

This is what we got for my mother: As many cans of tomatoes as we could find. More cans — creamed corn, baked beans, kidney beans, spaghetti. Pasta, as long as we could find packets that the weevils had not got into. A few packets of potato chips, for treats and when sick. A long brick of New Zealand cheese that my mother ran her hands over with pleasure when we brought it home. Tins of butter. One string bag of potatoes, one of garlic and one of onions: hopefully enough until we might restock with a shipment from Wamena, the large inland town not so far from Yuvut, or from someone's harvest that had not yet washed away. No beef, because all the options looked greyed and shrivelled. Two small chickens that we would try to keep frozen. Ten packets of bacon that we found hidden at the bottom of the supermarket's freezer. No fruit, because that, at least, was something plentiful in Yuvut. Mum also hoped there would be corn and green beans growing again once we got there. Two of the shampoos that looked familiar, because I thought Mum might like them (and she did). Ten boxes of milk powder that we would try to use before moisture got into them and turned them rancid.

When we unloaded at home, Dad pulled some chocolate out from behind his back and presented it to Mum. It was Toblerone and hard to find. Mum took it, squeezed his hand tight. Look at that, she said. We'll all share it.

Dad kissed her. The rain started again.

*Dear Grandad,*

*Sorry this is rushed. I am sending it now because we are at the post office in Jayapura and Dad thinks it will get to you faster than if I send it from Yuvut. I hope you and Grandma are having a good time in your new home. Does it have a garden or any animals? I hope it does. The rain has made all the plants grow really quickly here. One day there was only dust by the side of the road, and then after the rain came there were lots of green things. I don't know what kind of green things yet. Maybe you would know.*

*My friend Alyssa said that she did not know what her grandparents looked like when she went back to America one time. And they didn't know what she would look like either. I hope I will still know what you and Grandma look like when I get back one day. It might take a long time to get back, though. Please don't forget what I look like either.*
*Love, Ruth*

## THIRTY-FOUR

Circling above the Yuvut airstrip on our return felt familiar. The river below was full enough to cover its limestone scars but muddied brown as it hurried through the valley. The bump of the plane on the airstrip, the rush of the wing flaps as they worked to slow the plane down, the split-second quiet when the engine switched off before the unclipping of seat belts started: it all felt like something I knew now. Something that could be part of my knowing. We stepped out of the plane, just like we did on our first trip to Yuvut.

The door of the house was still light and flimsy. The house was a little dustier, a little more fragile than I remembered. Cockroaches scuttled under the furniture. The cicadas were louder. The rose had come back to life and at last bloomed (perhaps out of surprise at the rain), but we were too late for it and already the petals lay shredded at its feet. There were more holes in the floorboards. Two of the chickens had chicks. One had managed to keep five alive; the other had two left. Hawks and snakes, said Dad. It was a humid afternoon, and the bees thickly buzzing in the walls of the house and the grass that had gone to seed in the yard made me, too, feel thick and slow.

The rainwater tanks were full. We used damp rags to wipe the dust off each individual glass louvre, then I was allowed to run out of the gate to find Susumina, Yacob and the others. I left my shoes on the porch and took off, feet feeling all the dirt beneath their soles. I had filled my pockets with American candies to share. What would we do first? I wondered. Football, then creek? Creek, then hide-and-seek? Go to the river tomorrow?

But I did not even have time to run through the gate. Yacob was there waiting for me, with more of Susumina's younger relatives. He did not look well. There was sweat all the way round his collar.

Come, Yacob said. You have to see. It's Susumina.

# MAGNOLIA
*Baliem Valley, 1983*

*Magnolias existed on earth before the bees did, but in time for the beetles. This is what the German botanist tells Arice through his translator, when they stop to examine one growing over the path as they climb into the mountains. Arice tells the botanist (and me, on another day in Sentani) that this particular magnolia must be the offspring of one of the ones that an early missionary woman planted around her house further up the valley. That woman said they made her feel like she was back home in the Mississippi. Arice likes the flowers' heavy perfume as well, but thinks that their leaves look too plastic and the flowers are so delicate that they become soiled if even one petal gets bent or scratched.*

*The sky is overcast. Storm clouds bruise it, rolling down the steep sides of the mountains. They will have to hurry if they are to make it to the place where the botanist wants to camp before the rain catches up with them. Arice is only seventeen but when one of the pilots heard that a botanist was coming to the area, he recommended that she be the guide up the mountain. Arice's mother, before she died from tuberculosis, was one of the women who knew the forest best, including how to use things from it to heal. When she died, Arice took her place, so she knows best where the botanist might like to study.*

*In a gap in the clouds, the group can see where a mudslide has swept its way through trees and gardens. Tomi, the translator, explains to the botanist that there has been heavy rain all through the past week. This will make their path more difficult. Arice adds that the government contractors and logging companies are blaming the gardens of highlanders for the floods that washed away their camps earlier in the month.*

*'Yes,' says Tomi. 'But we say it was the loggers. It is the mountain's way. Sometimes it has to turn parts of itself bad so that it stays safe. Even soldiers are afraid to go up to its top.'*

*'Are you?' asks the botanist. Tomi shrugs and asks Arice. Arice shrugs. Arice does not plan on going to the bad places.*

*They all walk on. Tomi wears a red and black synthetic football shirt. There is a large tear under his armpit and wiry curls and sweat-glazed skin are visible through the gap. He is young like Arice, and not from her area. He learned his German from a priest down on the coast but must speak Bahasa Indonesia to Arice, which is a second language for both of them. Sometimes Arice thinks all of their words are like birds, flying out of their chests, and only sometimes reaching the right meaning.*

*The place they are walking towards lies in the mountains in the more empty end of the Baliem Valley. The year before, the same botanist went to different mountains, north of Papua's Mamberamo Basin, past swamps steaming with fetid pools of mosquito larvae and grey clay, past riverbanks tattooed with the tracks of crocodiles and wild pigs. He travelled with other scientists, documenting the presence of multiple species, living in a place that those on the expedition labelled a new 'Eden'. He says, now, to Tomi and Arice, that the Eden was far from exhausted, but he is seeking out more mountain flowers this time, to give his work on the region more breadth.*

*Arice knows the words used for Eden in her own language from church and literacy classes, where she learned to read the Bible. But she is not sure what the botanist means with his Eden, or how plants, other than forbidden ones, are a part of it.*

*But here they all are, descending through a film of mist into a miniature valley where Arice knows there is a bald space among some trees where tents can be staked and a hammock hung. She spots it at last and points it out to her companions. The mist is floating away, wafting further down the valley in long sucking white tentacles. The botanist is not the only scientist who has come to this area. A few years earlier, when Arice was just a girl and her mother was still alive, an Australian bird specialist made his way through. He was here, excited by the reports of other scientists that this might be the place to watch a gold-fronted bowerbird performing its elaborate dance. If he could just see this for himself, he told Arice's mother, then he could retire with a sense of accomplishment. They saw a number of birds on that trip (Arice's mother was one of the guides), but not that exact bowerbird. King birds of paradise, rosellas and tiny parakeets that catch their food on rocks — yes. The bowerbird and the scientist's sense of accomplishment remained elusive.*

*The botanist arrived by helicopter onto the airstrip closest to Arice's village. Its rotors caused leaves and twigs and skirts to whirl up and around as the botanist and Tomi leapt to the ground. Then the helicopter was gone, because the ground was too loose from the recent rains to risk being bogged down. Its chopping wind faded into the clouds until the cicadas' calls overtook it.*

*Now, as Arice leads the way, they reach the clearing in the trees. They stop, and are silent for a moment. The forest sounds as if it is alive with bells. The botanist fumbles in his backpack for a recorder. Tomi ambles to a fallen log and sits, looking at the surrounding trees with a mixture of curiosity and dislike. He prefers the wider spaces of the coast: the waves, the river mouths. Here, hemmed in by trees, one cannot guess when one might be snuck up on. He snorts and shoots a wad of mucus out of one nostril. It spatters on the forest floor and quickly disappears under a wave of insects who will not let even this small mark of humanity last for more than a few minutes.*

*'Look!' says the botanist, which does not need translation because he points to the end of the log where a small dark-brown echidna emerges. Tomi kicks at it and it scoots into the undergrowth. The botanist frowns but continues setting up his equipment: notebooks, drawing implements, magnifying glass, tweezers. Arice looks at his row of paints. The richness of their colours makes it seem like someone went through the forest, gathering up all the bright things, then boiled them down to become thick pastes for someone's notebook.*

*Then she sees something creamy-white peeking out from behind a larger tree. She goes over to look. Magnolia blooms spill their ruffles over the forest floor. 'Another descendant of the missionary one?' the botanist asks.*

*Arice is not sure this time, but it had to get here from somewhere. She shows the botanist the magnolia's tough bark and tells him through Tomi about its uses: for constipation, for the stomach, for fear. The botanist takes some notes, but is soon distracted by an orchid suspended in a tree nearby, its roots grasping through the air for something solid.*

*Arice starts building a small fire for boiling water and cooking their night's meal. The mist descends again. Soon it is hard for the botanist to see anything but ground ferns silhouetted against fog. Arice manages to get the fire going, despite the dampness. When it dies down and becomes coals, she buries sweet potatoes in it, and Tomi and the botanist join her, warming their hands. The sweet potatoes, once cooked, burn their tongues and fingers. They do not have many words to say, because it has been a day of too many words that do not quite meet in the middle. But they do laugh together when Tomi drops his first sweet potato. Then Arice, Tomi and the botanist feel their way to their own private spaces to sleep, each becoming alone in the mist.*

*While they sleep, I imagine that the smell of the magnolia creeps through to them all: for the botanist it means the stale perfume of a grandmother and his first visit to Kew Gardens. For Tomi, it means a different magnolia, petals dipped pink, outside the church by the coast where he went with the priest every Sunday and*

*Wednesday. For Arice, the magnolia scent speaks of both her mother and the missionary woman in her mother's memory. 'She gave me pills for malaria when I was pregnant,' Arice's mother said. 'They were good pills. But the woman was always lonely, always looking for the words that we could walk across to fix the gaps between us. Words that let us meet in the middle.' Arice, falling asleep, envisions one of the high rope bridges that her people might suspend to cross a river. Often just one rope tied above another, they swayed so low that they dipped into the current. The ropes sometimes broke. But people kept crossing them anyway.*

## THIRTY-FIVE

They told me Susumina was in her grandmother's hut and they did not try to stop me when I went in. She was laid out on a plastic mat on the floor and her grandmother flicked flies away with her skirt. Yellow foam crusted Susumina's lips and the edges of her nostrils. Like yellow coconut rice sold by the road, like stained tofu curds rising in a broth.

Fly spray, just like how her mother did it.

They were going to bury her tomorrow in a plywood box on the hill that faces the sun. With the babies, children, other girls who were pregnant too young.

Before I went into the hut I saw a man preparing a pig for its death. It was meant for the funeral feast, and the man stroked it, held it, brushed the dust from its sides. The pig shook, because maybe it knew, but still clung close to the man's legs, quivering between freedom without the man and death with him. I don't know what I would choose either, if it were me instead of the pig. With Julia I had three days' worth of warning that an ending was coming. With Susumina, none. Neither option is the easier one.

Choosing to drink fly spray means choosing to die slow. To die in days of sweat, with pains that bite barbed wire into the stomach.

There was a river high in the mountains to the east of Yuvut where unhappy women used to leap. For hundreds of years they jumped off a limestone rock that jutted out above the rapids. They jumped for a bad marriage, a dead child, a poor garden. They jumped for sick relatives, for unrequited love, for husbands who did not come home. They jumped for the same kinds of reasons that other people jump in other parts of the world. But now the river was not used, and the women chose fly spray instead. They knew it took days. They knew it shredded them raw before their lungs gave in.

I crouched with Susumina's grandmother by her body. A cousin sat by her head, cradling it while breastfeeding her own child, loose breast hanging free and low. Susumina wore a football shirt, complete with Ronaldo's name and number. She seemed smaller than she was when I left. A blanket was tucked around her legs. Her hands lay palms up, not clenched like I thought they might be. Her hair was braided tight against her head. Her aunts must have done that, because Susumina hardly ever wore her hair that way. Someone else had closed her eyes, and her lips were just partly open, as if she was about to speak.

Once I would have asked the grandmother why no one came for help, why no one tried to stop her, why this way of all ways. Why they let her groan in a corner, covering her with blankets, until it was over. I would ask what really happened to make her do this, try to find the story that is true.

But on this day I did not think I had the right to ask these questions, to decide that there had to be answers, to tell these stories of dead girls and claim that I knew all the details and could finish their stories. Julia's story, Susumina's. The only right I had to tell was by accident of birth, by the luck of my pulse. I could call fragments the whole story, but that would always be a lie. There would always be something missing that I did not know how to tell, could not know how to tell and should not.

Other women joined us one by one, kneeling with the body. Wailing began, my own inseparable from the rest. Where have you gone? the old women cried. Where have you gone? The hut filled with this wailing, with strands of song pulled out like rope attached to heavy, oh so heavy, weights from our insides. The hut's walls seemed to move with the sound. Maybe they might splinter. Maybe they might burst and maybe then our grief might find its way to Heaven. I was thrumming, humming, as if I was the inside of a drum.

They were going to bury her tomorrow in a plywood box on the hill that faces the sun.

## THIRTY-SIX

Sadly, that's what happens to many of them, said my father. These village girls. They get knocked up, or catch HIV from someone at one of their dances.

It can't be just that. Are you going to do anything about it?

What could I do, sweetheart? Can you put on some more toast for me?

I don't know. Said Yacob. Said Amin, said Yulimina, said Tias.

Policeman, said Susumina's grandmother, but nothing more.

This time my parents could not keep me from the funeral. They did not even try, perhaps because it was too late by the time they knew. I had already seen the body. But they did come with me. Mum walked the furthest from the house she ever had. I wore the shirt and shorts that Susumina had once admired: Minnie Mouse on the shirt, denim shorts.

Men sat in groups outside the hut, greeting every mourner as they arrived. Handshaking took two hands in Yuvut. They squeezed our hands, then moved up to our wrists, elbows, upper arms, and back down again. Not many words were said, but there were many of these handshakes. With each new arrival, the wailing began again. But on this day it seemed more like background noise, more like the music of a movie soundtrack and less like the main event itself. I started to see the difference between crying and wailing. Crying is what Susumina's grandmother, cousins, aunts were doing. Theirs was a raw and beating grief. Wailing was the scaffold upon which this grief could climb up into the clouds and far away from this place between the mountains. After an hour, I noticed that first my father, then even my mother, started to add their voices to the other voices: low but present. I saw that my voice, their voices, were wanted and needed, just like all the others, despite not being from Yuvut. No one told me not to cry. Nobody kept me from seeing the body, seeing everything.

Someone strung up a bright orange tarpaulin over the mourners as people spilled outside from the open doorway of Susumina's grandmother's hut. I sat between two older cousins, who started to show me how they made their string bags, while their voices changed from quiet wails to louder singing, depending on the flow of people in and out. My mother watched me with the cousins. Soon she sat with us, too, silent and watching the cousins' fingers move in the same motions over and over. Coloured rows of loose finger-knitting spread over their crossed legs. Jewel green, deep purple, Susumina's favourite red, Julia's favourite red.

Everywhere there was the smell of charred sweet potato skins and boiled rice, breath of the living and smoke from cooking fires. Our eyes stung with the smoke. By the end of the day, all our clothes would be steeped in that smoke smell, and it was days before the scent left our skin and stopped lingering around the airstrip.

The coffin was painted white. Susumina's body was lifted in her blanket by three men and placed in it. Again, I was surprised that she seemed so much smaller than I remembered or expected.

The burial was quick. The clay on the hill was loose from the rains and it made everything (the spades, hemlines, the soles of many feet) dark red. I stood with Yacob and Susumina's other relatives while her grandmother got into the grave with the coffin, calling for the men with the spades to bury her along with her granddaughter. The men let her cry and call and beat on the top of the coffin. Yacob clenched his hands over and over. The sound of the grandmother's cry rang out through the valley. The *polisi* stayed far away. Then the grandmother's sisters and living children stepped forward and pulled her out, keeping her close to their chests, letting her beat them with her fists, rubbing her back hard while their voices agreed with her. The wailing swelled. The grandmother's voice was high above the others, soaring, sobbing. The other voices, including my own, kept hers aloft, lifting higher and higher until the first dirt started falling on the coffin, and the voices finally subsided into low murmurings that did not stop all day. We were holding the dead close with these sounds, and only once all wailing, all murmuring, stopped could they be released to go where they pleased. I thought of Susumina and how she didn't know how to swim but she loved looking out at the depths of the river bends. I thought of Julia and wondered what was said at her funeral, how she was let go.

While they filled the grave, Susumina's grandmother fell to her knees, grasping in the dirt. The women with her spread their arms wide. We are here, they seemed to say. No one alone.

One of the church elders, Susumina's uncle, stood up and talked like he was in church. Lots of big stern words. Not everyone agreed with him, though, and soon there were multiple elders making comments across the grave. The women held each other and made their way back down the hill. There were many other graves up on the hill. Some of them were covered with small tin roofs to keep the rain from washing the mound flat. Some of their crosses were burnt in the fire, but some looked new. Some had nothing — just a rise in the ground if it was fresh, or a depression if it was very old.

Not only grief was felt on this day. As we walked back to Susumina's grandmother's place, I saw the young men, skin oiled with pig fat and cockatoo feathers in their hair, keeping to the edges and gripping their bows and spears tight. The night before, the ground shook with the beating of their bare feet as they got out their anger by running back and forth down the airstrip, singing hunting songs and hoping for permission to use their spears to seek answers and vengeance. But perhaps they already knew they were not going to get that permission this time, not when the rumours all involved a policeman with a weapon they were not allowed to have.

One of Susumina's slightly younger cousins, Dina, painted her face and arms with creek mud. As the funeral meal was prepared, she ran back and forth in front of the fence between Susumina's grandmother's house and the airstrip, waving a piece of wood and yelling that the spirit of Susumina now lives in her, breathes through her. As we passed on our way to the meal, she stopped running, shook my, my mother's and my father's hands hard, and then continued on her way. I wondered if I would know if Susumina's spirit ever went into me and if it would hurt.

The women put their grief back in their bags that were so wide they could hold the whole world. They put their grief in there for bringing out during late nights or early morning loneliness, and started opening the cooking pits. We sat in the grass that was already flattened from earlier in the day. Banana leaves appeared from somewhere, wide and long. The old men laid them in front of every group of people. We all sat in our family groups. Someone brought a plank out for my parents to sit on, perhaps noticing Mum's discomfort as she shifted in her skirt. The old men were also in charge of portioning out the meal. First the sweet potato leaves and other greens steeped dark with meat juices. Then the orange maize, the gold and amber potatoes, the tender stalks of a vegetable I had no English name for. Then the pig was spilt open and carved into large pieces with machetes. Here a foot, there an ear. The fat was soft and white. In a corner lay the already bare skull, chewed at by dogs that were constantly shooed towards the edges.

Whenever there was a funeral, a wedding, the opening of a building, or anything that involved more food than usual, there was one girl who always showed up. Her hair was wild and large, and she had very little clothing. When we first saw her we wondered which family she belonged to. When the meat was divided up among everyone, she did not sit with any family. But then each family, one by one, took some meat from their own pile and brought it over for her to eat. My father saw this and did the same. She ate fast but clean. When the food was gone, she left.

I remembered her from a Christmas Eve meal at the Indonesian church in Yuvut, early in our time in the village. That time we sat on wooden benches eating noodles and rice drenched in chilli powder, sipping chicken broth and gritty sweet coffee from bright orange mugs. The girl ate donated food then, too, keeping outside on the church's porch.

Who is she? I asked Yacob.

The girl who cannot speak, he said. We know she is an orphan but we don't know where she lives. We only see her when a pig is killed. She always knows somehow.

He pointed towards another woman at the edge of the gathering, bent over her own pile of donated food. See her? he said. She is a widow who only shows up at deathbeds. She lost all her children, all her family. She shows up to tell the spirits of the dead where to go. Heaven or Hell.

I watched the woman. She did not talk with anyone around her or seem to see anyone around her. She kept looking towards the mountains, and moved like she was impatient, nervous, ready to flee.

Heaven, I mouthed. Send her to Heaven. Send them all to Heaven.

## THIRTY-SEVEN

Once upon a time, the darkness scared the people of Yuvut. When the night bird sang its song, they rushed back into their huts because night time was the time when the spirits gathered. It was not a time for humans. But, times changed (as they do everywhere) and the young people of Yuvut began to slip out at night, meeting behind houses, in empty fields, on the crests of ungardened hills. They built bonfires to scare back the night, and danced and sang until dawn.

I thought that if I could get to one of these dances then I might understand more about what had happened to Susumina. Yacob knew a little about them. They weren't for people our age. They were for young people, bodies becoming full, straining towards something they did not know how to name. It was to one of these dances, Yacob said (after days of my questions), that Susumina had gone one night, then more, then too many.

It was at one of these dances that she met with the person who got her pregnant, very early pregnant, but still she knew she was pregnant enough to drink fly spray. At these dances, Yacob said, couples were not couples; Yuvut people and outsiders mixed, anything could happen. I asked him to watch and let me know when the next one happened. I did not know what to imagine except darkness and firelight, too much movement.

I slept little for four nights until there was a tap on my window. I looked out to see Yacob, washed grey in the moonlight. I tucked my shirt into my shorts to ward against the chill and other unnameable fears, and slipped out the side door. Elizabeth the cat watched from her place under a passionfruit vine, her eyes briefly flashing golden.

We did not have far to walk. Behind a building in the abandoned school yard there was a gathering of shadows, a fire at the centre. Laughter that seemed to take a physical shape. Men, boys with fuzz on their lips, shined bodies. Women, just skirt flickers in the dark. Someone had a ukulele; someone else had a bamboo mouth harp. Yacob and I held back now. We knew this was not a place for us. Not for Yacob, whose voice had not broken. Not for me, with my pigtails and Minnie Mouse. And again I felt like I was getting only a fragment of the stories happening here, only a tiny blurred fragment. But we watched. The moonlight slowly made the outlines of people more clear. I started to recognise people, or at least their voices. There was Dina, arms up, body swaying against one of the young contractors working on the road. There was a young woman who got married several months ago, talking in a corner with a man who was not her husband. Two shopkeepers, barely out of high school, leaned against the building, smoking and watching the girls. Someone passed around a soda bottle sawn in half. People grabbed it, bent their heads close and inhaled deep. Petrol, whispered Yacob. It was then that I noticed him shaking. Just a little, like the floorboards of our house whenever a plane landed or took off. Then I saw the policeman. He wore his uniform, too, like it made him proud, but his hat was off and sitting lopsided on a girl's head. He had his arm around her. I didn't know her until she turned her face up towards the sky and I saw that she was one of the girls who sat at the back of church, playing with the babies. I guessed that she was maybe three or four years older than me. Old enough to know how to look after babies, young enough to giggle too loud and play hopscotch after the service. The policeman twirled the hat on her head, kissed her. Yacob turned away.

Come on, he said. There is nothing else to see.

He walked me back to the house. I had forgotten how loud insects can be when you are outside at night among them. How they drown out all other thoughts, mask all other sounds, make you feel surrounded. I wanted to run like I ran that afternoon after the river bend, but Yacob did not seem to feel my same fear.

I lay awake for hours that night, breath not slowing. I used to imagine that life began with the advent of my own existence, that everything that came before consisted of blurred shapes moving in a white haze, and then life welled up like music from the gramophone my grandfather kept in the living room when the spindle (me) dropped into place. But in reality I dropped in, like any other child, halfway through the songs of some people's lives, at the end of others and some I missed completely. Susumina's timeline was not my timeline and I was not a protagonist in her story or song — just a small girl fighting for space in some of her ending chapters. The mosquito net around my bed that night felt too close and not close enough, not strong enough, all at the same time.

## SWEET POTATO
*Dadiwap, 1998*

The single mothers of Dadiwap have cleared a spot for their gardens in the place where the mists are heaviest in the mornings. It is always damp up there, squeezed on the mountainside, but that also means that their sweet potato leaves grow fast and dark, covering the dirt quickly and thickly. Their purple flowers greet the morning by opening with faces pointed at the sun as it breaks its way through the mist.

There is a cave in a valley, a day or two's walk from the women's gardens. It is not large. Just a crack in the side of the mountain, exposing its pale limestone, streaked with moss, to the daylight. This is where the first people came from. They walked out of the cave with five things: pigs, stone axes, bows and arrows, spears. And the sweet potato. These gifts came from the spirits and therefore have always been in the hands of the people, in their homes.

The single mothers of Dadiwap are single for different reasons. Yerema is single because her husband went to the city three years ago and never came back, leaving her with two children. She is not sad about this. He used to send her and the children new clothes and sweets, but nothing comes now. She is not waiting for anything or for him. Her children, both girls, are almost strong enough to help in the gardens, and when she goes home it is peaceful not to have to worry about a man's coming and goings. She is the one who first went to the other single women and suggested they all have their gardens together. There is a tree near the centre of the gardens that they will not cut down or burn. Under the tree they, or their older daughters, take turns watching the younger children who move too much or are too sick to swing on their mothers' backs in a noken as she bends and weeds. Yerema's children are too old now to swing on her back, and sometimes she misses the weight of them so much that she borrows a baby from another mother who needs time free from the constant tug and swing on her forehead and shoulders.

Rossina's husband also went away, but not to the city. The Indonesian military know all about

*Dadiwap men. They know that some Dadiwap men chafe and shift against the military closing in on every side. The Dadiwap men know that there is some safety in the forest. A year ago there were shots fired from the trees at soldiers. A soldier died, more were injured. Witnesses saw nobody but heard the sound of running feet everywhere. They saw a large bird in a tree, one they did not recognise. Rossina knows it was her husband and that he was the one, or one of the ones, who fired on the soldiers. She is proud of this and tells her young son, who has never seen his father, about it at night when they both cannot sleep. She watches the dark sides of the mountains when she is sleepless and wonders which part of the forest her husband melted into. He will be full OPM now, the guerrilla group that wants freedom. Part of her imagines them, all those missing men and some women, massing in the forest somewhere together. Making an army that will one day sweep over a mountain ridge and devour the soldiers whole. But the other part of her knows that her husband may be alone, or just with a few men, and that they might be spread so thin that most of the OPM do not even know where the others are.*

*Kimbe is single because she always has been and also because she wants to be. Before Yerema started these gardens, she sat in the doorway of her house, babies all around, and wondered if she might ever break out of those walls. Now she bends in the sweet potato vines and sometimes breaks apart clay with her fingers just because she likes the way it crumbles in her hands, the steamy breath of damp dirt in warm sun. She is pregnant again and the women have all given her their advice. The last time she gave birth she was alone, because her mother died long ago, but this time she will be surrounded with mothers. There are the widowed mothers, too. The ones who lost their husbands or boyfriends to landslide, malaria, tuberculosis and other unnameable things.*

*The gardens are not easy. To get there they all walk a narrow track that eats its way up the mountain. Sometimes the gardens flood, sometimes the ground rots the potatoes in their beds before they can be unearthed. Sometimes disease gets to the vines, sometimes there are thieves.*

*But after their morning's work, the women walk back to their houses together, children tugging on skirts, on hair, on shoulders. By this time of day the sun has baked the path that was dew-soaked hours earlier. It splits to its edges and shows the birds where the worms are hiding. Grasshoppers hurl themselves in front of the advancing women and children, delirious with movement and sunshine. Down below, someone is keening. A woman's husband was sick last night with an infection that went to his chest. The single mothers look at each other, knowing. They adjust their string bags on their foreheads, feeling the just-harvested potatoes move with their bodies. Tonight they will roast some of them in coals, and keep the others for market. Yerema fixes a knot in her youngest daughter's hair. Another woman brushes dirt from Yerema's eldest's back, where she was lying in the grass, playing with a toddler. An old woman waits for them at the end of the path, just before their houses. She is too weak to climb to the gardens any more. She grabs one of the children to wipe his nose and slaps another who is crying. Yerema smiles. What news? she asks the old woman. Late afternoon is approaching and the mist is descending again, hiding the women's gardens in its folds.*

## THIRTY-EIGHT

A few days after the funeral, my mother asked if she could walk with me down to the river. I said yes and we went, but not as far as the bend. Just where we could feel the cool air coming down over the rapids and watch people set their fish traps. Mum did not say much on the way down and not much on the way back. But the spleen-space inside me, cracked open yet again by Susumina's death, ached and waited, and for the first time I wondered if I could take her to the bend — Next Time, a time that could actually happen This Time. Susumina's death told me that maybe this spleen-space would never be the same again, but maybe it was not supposed to be either. I waited and watched my mother.

Perhaps we thought we could slip back into life in Yuvut like we were always part of it, like we never were away. But we were not the same and Yuvut had not stood still either. And, as the hospital neared completion, empty and silent like a church, there were rumours cracking and buckling under the ground that had grown dry between rains again.

The rumours took two shapes. First, two men went missing. These were not important men. Both were glue sniffers with no wives, no families. Somehow they had become untethered from those kinds of things, though one was claimed as a distant cousin of the head pastor and both knew which clan they fell into. They were not friends. They had no permanent home. One spent most of his time behind the empty school with his glue and sometimes petrol. The other preferred to wander down by the river. Yacob said that one was crazy. He did look like it. Something had dragged one part of his face down by its corners and frozen it into a permanent grimace, as if he were in pain.

But people did notice, slowly, when they were no longer there. At first it was the river man. Two of the fishermen used to give him the smaller parts of their catch, or share palm wine with him once in a while. Then the pastor noticed that his cousin was no longer calling out Brother! Brother! from behind the school on Sundays when he passed him by. Once their absence was noticed, everyone saw the spaces they had filled. They could not un-see the spaces.

It was some of the older boys who started the rumour about how they disappeared. The boys hung around with the contractors who were working on building a bridge for their new road. The boys heard from these contractors that it was the practice, in some parts that fell in or rimmed the Pacific Ocean, to bury the bodies, or at least the heads, of people in the foundations of new buildings or structures like bridges, so that their bodies would make the structures strong as the flesh and bones rotted beneath. Ah, said the fishermen. It was as that new bridge's foundations were laid that the men disappeared. Ah, said the women, and spread that around their gardens and husbands. Ah, said their husbands, and passed it on to the pastor, who announced it at church. No, said the contractors, but it would not make a difference what they said now.

Nothing had happened yet, but the contractors locked their doors at night and young men started talking more around their fires. The bridge washed away in the first heavy rain after it was built. It's because the men who were in its foundations were weak, said the boys. They needed soldiers or policemen in those foundations to hold them fast. They said this loud, so that the soldiers and policemen could hear. The boys then ran off laughing to smoke.

The hospital's foundations were not free from scrutiny either. Dad came home one day, saying that someone had been digging under the concrete corners, looking for something. Mum started to have dreams of people bursting through the earth. Like zombies, said Dad.

No, not like that. Like sprouts in a garden, like bamboo shoots pushing.

I'm sorry, said Dad.

Oh, I wouldn't say it's a frightening dream. I'm not sure what kind of a dream it is. But not a frightening one.

The other rumour was draped around the upcoming elections for governor of the region. The former *bupati* was running again.

His opponent was hopeful. Under the former there was the drought, the killings of people running to helicopters for famine food, the disappearances of men who might be the kind of men who slipped out in the middle of the night to talk about forbidden things like their own flag and independence. The bupati met Suharto once, and the photo of the meeting had rich red drapes in the background and just the smallest glimpse of someone pushing a cart piled high with food. Now that Suharto was no longer Suharto, the tune had changed slightly. The former bupati travelled through villages as if they were links on a chain, all bringing him closer to his second term. He handed out money in thick wads on these visits. You want a school, I'll build you a school, he said. You want a shopping mall? You want a road? How about a train? An airport? Anything you want!

He was about to visit Yuvut. But, in just the past few days, something had happened to the bupati's single opponent. A heart attack, said the Indonesian newspapers. Suspicious, said the one Australian newspaper which noticed and a random amnesty group based in Singapore. Poison, said the opponent's closest friend, the man who was ready to step into his shoes. So this was the kind of talk closing in around Yuvut as the bupati's aeroplane closed in, too.

When it landed, it seemed that everyone in Yuvut was down at the airstrip. I stood with Yacob by the fence. We got there early to be close, and passed the time scraping pictures on a boulder with a stick and listening to the talk around us as it grew and grew. I saw my father towards the back of the crowd. He saw me and tried to move closer, but the people were too many so he just waved.

Because it was the thing to do, the people of Yuvut had prepared a welcome party. About forty men and forty women stripped to their waists, the women still wearing bras. One or two men wore the penis gourd of past days, but the rest wore shorts. The women put on their grass skirts that they usually kept hanging up for old grandmothers' sakes. The bupati preferred to see everyone dressed in what he called 'authentic' gear, they had been told. On their heads they wore feathers: russet cassowary, arranged in a ring. A yellow fountain of bird of paradise, standing tall. Gem-like parakeet feathers, pure-white cockatoo, iridescent bodies of dead bowerbirds, mouths that could never speak again wide open to the sky. Woven armbands, stuffed with feathers too, squeezed biceps. The welcome party waved large palm fans, transforming into birds as they advanced on the airstrip. Swish went the fans. Stomp went their feet. Their voices called high, repeating the same sounds, not words, over and over again until they started to become part of my own thoughts. Yacob swayed along with them. I saw my mother come down the path from the house and wait on the very fringe of the crowd, shirt buttoned up to her throat but skirt swishing full. Two women nodded to her, reached out their hands.

When the bupati's plane landed there was a hush for a second while the propellers beat against the wind, finally slowing into silence. Then the plane's door opened and a leather-covered foot emerged. The welcome party launched into their welcome. They danced forward, then a little back, forward again. Their wave advanced on the plane, singing as the bupati, a member of the military and another man in government uniform stood in front of the plane, hands folded over bellies, watching the welcome with smiles under their moustaches. Their bellies stretched wide under shirts that pulled, fighting belts and buttons.

The welcome party stopped with a shout when their song was done. Sweat lined the shoulder blades of the men closest to me.

The clay the women had used to paint designs on their stomachs and faces cracked and bled with sweat into their creases and folds. A church elder stepped forward to formally announce Yuvut's welcome. The bupati shook his hand, but then turned towards the crowd, cutting the church elder off. There was a rustle that swept through the crowd all the way to its edges.

Yacob sucked air through his teeth. Big man, he said. Not as a compliment.

The bupati talked loud and long in government language. There was no translation for the old women, the old men, who might find that language twisted and tangled in their ears. They stayed watching, though. The women's hands kept moving, kept knitting at those ever-growing bags. The bupati talked about the usual stuff that governors trying to be governors again talk about. Money, jobs, new schools. Healthcare, unity, new airstrips. His voice droned; we all continued to sweat. I watched tiny brown butterflies feeding on a teenage girl's sweat patches and some more settling on a dog turd on the footpath.

When the bupati finished, people were not sure if he was properly finished or not, but then they noticed that he was just standing there, so they all clapped, except for the younger children who were already leaving the crowd like ants hunting for food. Their mothers rolled their eyes.

Because this visit was a bupati's visit and because it was election campaign time, there was then a feast. The usual screams of pigs had rung out across the airstrip that morning and the rocks had baked in the coals for hours. The bupati walked through the rows of cooking pits, shaking the hands of women checking on their food. When it was time to eat, though, we all sat in the grass, peeling off the cracked skins of sweet potatoes in long crusted strips, while the bupati sat inside one of the government administration buildings, eating noodles and boiled chicken with chillies. Some of the Yuvut men went in to him, where he sat with some of the contractors and other government workers, bringing him a pile of cubed pig fat piled high on a banana leaf. I wanted to see if he would eat it, but too many other children stood around the door, scuffing bare feet into the footprints left behind by government shoes. Dad and I ate around the cooking pits, then took home meat and taro, my mother's favourite kind of Yuvut food.

I figured that the day was pretty much over then. Bupati had come, seen, and would most likely get elected, whether Yuvut voted for him or not. I climbed a tree with a *Famous Five* book we inherited from a tiny international school that closed a few mountains over. All afternoon there had been voices rippling their way from the airstrip and the churchyard with the cooking pits over to our house. But then, as I began reading the first chapter of my book, there was yelling. Several men came running up from the creek where they had been washing, towels askew, skin still wet, curious about the yelling. I followed them down to the airstrip.

The bupati, his military man and his administration man were all sitting in the plane, waiting to go with the doors shut. The pilot stood outside trying to talk with the yelling people, but no one was listening.

I found Yacob. Money, he said. The bupati didn't give the elders nearly the same amount as he gave to Gimbis the other week.

The pilot waved his arms. No one listened. I saw the bupati's head inside the plane, bent forward as if he were praying or reading or sleeping.

The yelling talk stopped as it had started, but not because the people had given up. Men began running to the plane.

Welcome-party men and regular men wearing their everyday clothes. They could not have guns, but sometime during the afternoon they had gone home and collected their spears and bows. I looked for the policemen, not because I was afraid but because I was wondering. They stood in their blue and red near the church, always watching. The men, upon reaching the plane, divided in a stream around it, running, running. The plane was a lone island in the centre as the men eddied around it. A child, maybe two years old, stumbled forwards towards the stream. A man bent down and swept him up out of the feet and on to his shoulders. He kept running, the child smiling and waving. The bupati's shoulders looked tense, still. The pilot was not waving his arms now, just waiting for the bodies to slow and stop. Men whipped spears centimetres from his face. He sweated. Another man broke from the mass with his longbow, placed an arrow in it and pulled back. The bupati looked up now. The bowman and the bupati stared at each other. The man with the bow looked until the bupati turned away, and then the man stepped back into the swirl of other men and was lost in the anger that was travelling through them all and spinning out into the crowd, throughout Yuvut.

Bodies, bodies everywhere. I was pressed with them, all skin to skin, feeling the same anger but also feeling as though I was on the outside, trying to reach my way in. Like it was not my place to see.

The police stepped forward now and fired over the heads of the running men. A woman somewhere screamed. The men's running slowed, then stopped, then they left, spreading down many paths out of the village and towards the mountains. I saw a man who looked like one who once came out of the forest to knock on our door in the middle of the night. He said then that he was hiding because he killed somebody and their family wanted revenge. He came for malaria medicine, which my mother gave him, hands not even shaking. I remembered that detail. He had machete scars down his back. As the men dispersed, I saw a scarred back disappear with them, and wondered if it was the same man and where he might sleep that night.

The plane's engines finally started, pushing the last of the crowd back towards the fence. The plane left, the mountains absorbing the last of its engine drone, and the last of the fighting songs of Yuvut's young men faded with it.

I went back inside the house. My mother stood still by the window. She had seen what had happened.

That night I heard my mother speaking to my father: Gunshots, Isaac. Gunshots.

I know.

You don't know. No one knows how to talk about gunshots.

## THIRTY-NINE

Maybe you do not need to know how to talk about gunshots, because gunshots are unspeakable things. A Yuvut boy got shot high in the thigh and once through the shoulder on this night, but did not die.

OPM, said the police. A double-crossing messenger between two sides at war.

Police, said everybody else. A double-crossing messenger between two sides at war.

The boy's mother did not talk about this shooting at first. She softened the edges of the wound with tea leaves, rubbed sugar and salt into the wound and, when that did not work, tobacco juices that she chewed herself. The wound did not improve but grew darker, swelled, and then its smell turned over into something that made the boy's mother hold her breath and the boy believe he was already half-rotted, half-buried in the ground.

That is when the boy's mother told. She and her sisters stayed up all night, crying and begging for his life.

And all the while the policemen tightened their grips on their guns and they looked towards the mountains, and voices jumped and hissed across the radio waves.

Finally, a pilot brought my parents a letter.

Security Threat Escalated, it said. Evacuation Recommended.

My parents were calm. We packed our one book, the dental floss, medications, passports. I did not take Patches, Matilda or Brown Eyes. I lined them up on the pillow underneath the mosquito net and left them behind, their eyes pointed towards the dream-catcher that I also left hanging. My father took one more trip back to the hospital that was close to being finished but never would be by him. I went with him. The hospital sat in a patch of bare land, looking like it was uncomfortable to be there but was going to make the best of it.

Then we went down to the plane with our bags, much smaller this time. Some people shook our hands as we left. Yacob came running up to me. He waved, told me to say hi to Ronaldo if I saw him. I promised I would, and asked that Yacob would do the same for me. As we crossed from the fence to the plane, there was a rush of voices. Four men came up, carrying a stretcher made from rice sacks. On it lay the boy who was shot. The policeman by the shed stood up. The boy's mother came running behind the men, calling to the pilot to take her child out of Yuvut to the hospital on the coast where he might be saved. The pilot looked at us. My parents nodded.

Just like that we were all loaded into the plane with our things. At the last minute, the boy's mother climbed in with him, after her sister passed her a lipstick stub and a trussed live chicken for the journey. Just like that we were humming down the airstrip at full speed, the plane's engine erasing us from Yuvut's landscape as if we were pencil marks on the dirt.

One. Only one, only one, said Dad, above the engine. He put his head in his hands. We were supposed to build the hospital, he said. We were supposed to save so many.

We weren't ever going to save anyone from anything, said Mum. We just thought we were.

Outside the plane there was a leaf clinging to the wing. Inside, the boy's sinking, stinking flesh made us cover our mouths and noses with our shirt collars, sick bags. I thought of Julia, of hospital masks, of the stories that could not get spoken and the ones that do and the gaps between them. Away, away we went from Yuvut and the mountains and the deepening, deepening river bend.

As we flew up and out with the boy on his stretcher, my mother's hand steady around his un-shot leg, we did not know where we might be going but we were up in the clouds where there might be a God, even if we could not recognise him. In the sky, where there is no sickness, and death is withheld for a moment. In the sky, where things are too clean. And I looked down and I saw the last of the river bend before it was squeezed between the mountains. I looked at my mother, and she was looking, too.

Because I did, in the end, take my mother to the river bend. The day before the plane took us away, when the memory of gunshots was still too fresh for us all. I told her, You remember those stories about the taniwha that lived in the river down below Mr Ashton's pond? And she remembered. I said, Maybe there's another one, or the same one, living in the river bend here, too. Let's see.

And I had the same feeling as I had with Julia and the Tinies — Please make her believe. Everything would be okay if she would only believe. And then there we were. Down by the river, the last day Yuvut was with us. Mum and I with our feet in the shallows because it was hot and we sweated through our clothes and sunscreen the whole walk downriver. Fish under the surface splashed ripples in our direction.

Taniwha, I said.

Is she a nice taniwha? asked Mum.

Sometimes. She is a monster, you know.

I always thought they were guardians, Mum said.

I bet they can be both, I said.

We went back to the bank and sat. I started pulling prickles out of the hem of Mum's skirt that she wore even though I told her shorts were better. She pulled prickles out of my shorts because they collected prickles anyway. She started singing, very quiet: *You know I love you, you know God loves you* . . . She hummed the rest. I thought about the cat, Elizabeth, and how hard she fought against my hold on the night the burial hill burned. Seeing my mother there, on the rocks, sweat-shined, reminded me that she was human, could bleed. I thought about timelines again and wondered where I was on Mum's timeline and what I must look like to her. She had freckles across her collarbone and nose, and I decided one day my hair would turn dark like hers. She was beautiful, I saw that then, and I knew that she was beautiful every day, because children like to believe that about their mothers.

Before we walked back we saw a kingfisher perched right above the bend. Its feathers were the bluest of blues and I did not know how we had not seen it earlier. I thought of Dina and of Susumina's spirit and how spirits could go into the birds or the fireflies, too. My mother whistled to the kingfisher. It looked at her, opened its wings for a moment. I did not know what type of kingfisher it was. I might or might not be able to find it, corner it in my guidebook. Susumina, Yuvut, Papua: none of them could be cornered and defined in a letter for my grandfather. And nor would my mother. Sometimes all we can do is watch, have our own eyes to the earth even if we do not always know what we are seeing. I wanted the full stories of Julia dying, and then of Susumina dying, to make my life solid again. But they did not. Instead it was the reaching out of Susumina's hand, the thread of a cry from my mother's throat in chorus with someone else's sorrow, the stretch of many types of grief that spin out across Papua's throbbing bird body and across the world. I did not know if the word Divorce was still a thing my mother thought about, but —

There we were, down by the river, where we could each look at the other and see. See Miriam, not just mother. See Ru, not just sister-less. I breathed in the dark scent of the river and my mother. There was a certain thickness of sunlight. Somewhere there was a buzz of warm.

## THE LAST WORD
### *New Guinea Oak*

*In an American pamphlet on choosing timbers for home DIY and other projects:* 'New Guinea Oak is a good economical replacement for American White Oak. It is useful for flooring, cabinets, handrails, bridges, paneling, cladding, plywood construction. The grain is attractive. Wood can be prone to termite and borer attack if not removed from the forest promptly.'

*The women of Yuvut sing:* We know how river and fire can take, how they both wash across the ground until there is nothing.

*The loggers are coming, coming, coming. So are the rains. So are the military, the police, the miners and the scientists. Women build fences to protect their children. They build them around their gardens to try to keep them from washing down the mountains, because the roots of the trees are no longer there to hold the earth together.*

*Women of Yuvut:* We, too, know.

*There is a thrumming and a stirring in the earth. The mountains speak. The trees speak with the mountain, their moans carried through the valleys.*

*Women of Yuvut:* We know.

*The birds, too, add their voices. They carry the voices of the women and the trees and the mountain up and away, flinging them to every corner of the earth.*

*Women of Yuvut:* We know.

*The earth holds other movements, other voices, layered upon each other like primordial sediment. It can no longer hold in its bullets, its bones, its bodies. They are waking, they are moving, they are pushing and clambering with each other to wind their way up the broken bodies of trees and mountains, towards the clear air.*

*Women of Yuvut:* We know, we know.

*There is speaking, there has always been speaking. There is a breaking through.*

## AUTHOR'S NOTE

This is a work of fiction set at a particular time in West Papua's history. Many of the events described are real events or inspired by real events, but I have taken liberties with them and their timelines for the sake of the story. Their telling comes with the gaps, idiosyncrasies and manipulation that memory and narrative bestow. The characters, too, are inventions, and I have fictionalised the names of some locations.

A brief note on terminology. From 1973 to 2001, West Papua was known as Irian Jaya. The Indonesian government now administers the western half of New Guinea as two provinces, called Papua and West Papua (Papua Barat), instead of one. However, most Papuans inside and outside Papua prefer to use the terms 'Papua' and 'West Papua' interchangeably to refer to the whole western side of the island as one, and I have done the same in this book to respect that preference.

Many people in many places have helped *The Earth Cries Out* come into existence. Massey University was my writing home for five years, and my teachers there helped me grow as both a writer and a reader. Thank you especially to Thom Conroy for first telling me I could write, and then supervising the early stages of this book. Thanks to the New Zealand Society of Authors (NZSA) for placing me with Daniel Myers in their tertiary mentorship programme. This opportunity gave me the motivation to continue with the book when I thought about putting it aside. A month in Peter and Dianne Beatson's house at Foxton Beach gave me space and time to work in 2014.

An early version of the first chapter of this book appeared under a different name in the *Dominion Post* in January 2014. A variation of one of the plane crash scenes was also published by *takahē* magazine (issue 80, 2013) in my short story 'Another Side of White'.

Andrew J. Marshall and Bruce M. Beehler's *The Ecology of Papua* was an invaluable resource on Papuan botany. I borrowed a quote for my 'Orchid' chapter from Ernst Mayr's 'A Tenderfoot Explorer in New Guinea' (1932), which I found in *The Essential Naturalist* (2011, 263). I also include a quote from Johann David Wyss's *The Swiss Family Robinson*.

I have inflicted drafts of this book on a number of friends over the years. Special thanks go to: Talia Greyson, Fran Atkinson, Heather Reasbeck, Kate Dalley, Hannah Gibson, Sam Botz, Katie Blankenau, Ilana Larkin, Delali Kumavie, Mlondi Zondi and Tyrone Palmer. Thank you for not leaving me alone with my writing. Thank you to my editor, Jane Parkin, for helping this book be the best it can be. And many, many thanks to Harriet Allan at Penguin Random House New Zealand for believing in this book and helping me believe in it, too.

Thank you to my parents for taking their children to live in a village in the mountains on an island shaped like a bird. Thank you for teaching me how to listen to stories and for being nothing like the parents in this book. That village became the first home I knew. Thank you to the people there who made it so, and for telling me stories. I want to especially thank Pilem M., who told my father a version of the story of the hornbill, and the late Abok M., who told the story of the woman who got lost. Wa, Nasini. Wa, wa, wa.

Thank you to Josh Eastwood, the boy I fell in love with in the shadow of Mt Cyclops. Thank you for following me across the oceans, for your patience, for keeping me steady.

BJE